Deacon made a beeline for Ellie, making her stomach somersault

"Hey, gorgeous." Hand casually about her waist, he bent to deliver a platonic kiss to her cheek. *Why was she wishing for more?*

"Hey, yourself. Glad you could make it."

"Looked dicey for a bit, but considering the fancy hair you're sporting, it was worth the effort."

Like a giddy teenager, Ellie's spirit soared at the compliment.

"Stop. My hair always looks like this."

He snorted. "I don't know what mirror you've been looking in, but I haven't seen you look this hot since...well..." He whispered in her ear, giving her shivers, "Since that time back when—" She reddened, and he had the good grace to look away and clear his throat. "But we probably shouldn't discuss that here."

Cheeks still flaming, she elbowed him before leading the way to their seats. When he squeezed her hand, she squeezed back. Her usual guilt was there, but so was something else she hadn't felt in a long time—anticipation for what might be next to come.

Dear Reader,

Never have I written a story more about family—not just blood ties, but the relationships we form with friends and coworkers and the entire network of people who comprise the colorful quilts of our lives.

If you've read any of my books, you know I adore kids of all ages. In real life I'm pretty much the same. I'm honored that my kids' friends are usually mine, too, and once I learn their struggles, I add those to my already full worry list.

Deacon Murphy spends a large portion of this book struggling to figure out if he's even capable of love. Love for his family and friends and most especially Ellie, his best friend's widow.

With the recent loss of my last surviving grandparent, my blood family has grown perilously small, yet the more friends I make, the more reassured I am that since they, too, count as family, I will never be truly alone.

My daughter's friend Louisa is having a baby and I find myself more and more excited to welcome this little boy or girl into the world. That, in turn, makes me excited for when my kids start having kids. *Eeeek!* (But not too soon! LOL!) By the time this story hits shelves, I will have held this new addition to our extended family and in doing so, will have found a whole new person to love.

Whomever you count as your family, give them a hug!! And cross your fingers for Deacon to figure out what love means to him, before it's too late….

Happy reading!

Laura Marie

A SEAL's Secret Baby

LAURA MARIE ALTOM

HARLEQUIN®
entertain, enrich, inspire™

Recycling programs
for this product may
not exist in your area.

ISBN-13: 978-0-373-75419-9

A SEAL'S SECRET BABY

Copyright © 2012 by Laura Marie Altom

Chapter One

Tell him.

Ellie Hilliard caught herself staring at Deacon, her dead husband's best friend. He stood at the surf's edge, glaring at the angry Atlantic. For August, it was a gloomy, miserable day. The rest of the crowd gathered at her in-laws' to commemorate Tom's life was inside, clustered about the big screen TV, which flashed home videos of happier times. Family clips had been merged with lighter moments shared with his Navy SEAL team. The worst to bear were intimate scenes caught with him and his daughter. Hard to believe a year had already passed since Tom had been gone.

The rain had stopped, but wind still whipped Ellie's hair. Holding it back, and kicking off her heels at the foot of the beach house stairs, she picked her way through saw grass on the dune and then across the beach. Seagulls shrieked over a find farther down the shoreline.

Reaching Deacon, she said, "We need to talk."

"'Bout what?" At six-four, he towered over her by nearly a foot. His black hair was cut in a military buzz, and his square jaw was as hard as his muscled body. Tom used to say once you got to know him, Deacon was a big softie. Ellie had known him in the most intimate way a woman could. He'd led her to a dangerous ledge, then had urged her to jump....

She wanted to spill everything, but found her pulse racing to an uncomfortable degree.

"Ellie! Deacon!" Tom's father, John, stood at the deck railing, hands cupped to his mouth. "Dinner's ready!"

Ellie's spirits both soared and deflated. It had taken her a while to work up the courage to tell Deacon her most closely guarded secret. This latest interruption had been hell on her emotions.

He sighed. "Guess we better head for the house."

"Deacon, wait." Instinctively reaching out, she clasped his forearm, only to just as quickly draw away. Considering their past, touching him was never a good idea. "We really do need to talk."

"Later." His back was already turned, and his size allowed him to take one step for three of hers.

Swallowing her disappointment, Ellie doggedly followed.

Deacon wasn't even supposed to be here. Well, he'd been invited, but no one had expected his team to have returned from their latest mission.

Deacon had come to her after Tom's funeral, explaining that as his friend had lay dying, he'd asked Deacon to watch after Ellie and his one-year-old daughter, Pia. Each week, Deacon faithfully mowed the lawn and performed light maintenance on the Cape Cod house. When he was off on a mission, he arranged for a lawn company to tackle outside chores. He even insisted on regularly changing her car's oil. In the physical sense, Deacon worked hard to live up to the promise he'd made. But emotionally?

He barely spoke to her. Probably a good thing, but it still bothered her. Why, she couldn't have said. It just did.

Entering the house, she and Deacon joined the crowd of just over forty seated around the dining room table and folding tables, which had been draped in Tom's favorite color, royal blue. Tom's father stood, raising his champagne. "Helen and I didn't invite all of you here to mourn our son, but rather to celebrate his amazing life. We want you to rejoice, as we do, in the blessings of his daughter, Pia, and dear wife, Ellie. On this anniversary of his…"

When John's voice cracked, Helen put her hand on his shoulder. "I think what my husband is trying to say is thank you. Words can't express how much comfort it brings us, knowing our son was loved. So here's to Tom."

All assembled raised their glasses.

The dinner proceeded. Helen had hired a caterer for the occasion and the Italian food Tom loved soon had everyone in high spirits, swapping humorous stories about Ellie's late husband, and in general trying to make the best of the tragedy of a young life taken.

A few times during the meal Ellie felt Deacon's gaze on her. But when she looked at him, he'd glance away. The one time their eyes did meet, she flashed a faint smile, and he did the same.

Pia, who was almost two, sat in her high chair beside Helen. The toddler was adored by her grandparents, which made Ellie's secret all the harder to bear.

By the time they had eaten their fill, the clouds had broken, and the majority of Tom's SEAL family headed outside for beach volleyball. Unfortunately for Ellie, Deacon got caught up in the game.

Had she been wrong in thinking that having him with her today of all days was a sign? That she'd held on to her secret long enough?

Pia had hauled all her favorite beach toys from the box Helen kept on the deck. Her giggles rode on the wind when the seawater she poured into her sandcastle moat pooled for a moment, then vanished. "Gone, Mommy!"

"I know, sweetie. Funny, huh?"

"Yeah…" She was already engrossed in trying the trick again.

Ellie wished she could enjoy the simple pleasure of playing with her daughter, but for whatever reason, telling Deacon seemed to have taken on crushing importance. She'd heard through the SEAL wife grapevine that this latest mission had been brutal. By the grace of God, the team had all returned home safely, but what if they hadn't been so lucky?

How would she live with herself, knowing two men had died without learning a truth they'd both been entitled to hear?

DEACON MURPHY MADE A POINT OF avoiding Ellie and her daughter like the plague. He'd promised his best friend, Tom, that he'd watch over them, and to the very best of his abilities, he did just that.

The night Tom had died, they'd been in Afghanistan, taking care of business the way SEALs know how, when from out of nowhere enemy fire had started raining down as if hell had sprung a leak. The night had been so black, their faces and gear so well camouflaged, it'd taken precious seconds for Deacon to even see blood pulsing from his buddy's neck. He'd loved the man more than he loved his own brother. He and the rest of their team had finished the mission, then carried Tom's lifeless body eighteen miles across rugged terrain to their rubber combat craft, which they'd partially buried on the beach.

The whole way, Deacon had fought dark, drowning emotions he hadn't been equipped to handle.

Now, with Virginia Beach sunshine boring a hole through his head, he felt Ellie sitting on the sidelines, watching his every move, no matter how hard he tried distracting himself with the game. The two of them had their own special dance—the avoidance shuffle. Even though she'd married Tom, it had been Deacon who'd known her first. Known her in every way a man can know a woman, at least physically.

The ball came at him, but his reaction time was off.

"What the hell, Buns?" his pal Garrett complained. Lord, Deacon hated the name all of his buddies called him—especially when they were pissed. On weekend leave from BUD/S, it hadn't escaped their notice that base bunnies seemed to enjoy that particular portion of Deacon's anatomy. "That was for the win."

"Sorry. Guess my head's not in it."

While his team brokered a deal for the best out of three games to win bragging rights, Deacon headed into the house for fresh beer. He was careful to walk the long way around Ellie and her daughter. He couldn't imagine what she wanted to talk with him about, and he honestly didn't want to know.

Much the same way it'd been hammered into him to

shut out physical pain, Deacon did the same with the emotional wounds of Tom's passing.

Tom Hilliard had been the best man he had ever known, a hero in every sense of the word. He would blast through bad guys, only to then save their starving dogs. Everyone had loved Tom, which was why Deacon had introduced him to Ellie. She might have been the best lay he'd ever had, but she was also deeply spiritual and intrinsically good. Soft-spoken, and tender enough to have kissed his battle scars. Deacon was a surface dweller who didn't believe in getting too far under anyone's emotional skin. Connecting with his SEAL team was one thing, but women? Not for him.

Truth was, he wasn't even sure why he'd come to this thing for Tom. Maybe out of respect for his friend's folks. Deacon hated swapping stories, or talking about how Tom was in a better place. Screw that. Tom's heaven had been with Ellie and little Pia.

When she approached this time, Deacon again tried to dodge her.

"Deacon, wait," she said, grasping his arm.

Lips pressed tight, he stared into the blue sky, rather than look her in the eye.

"T-thank you for being here."

"Sure."

"Thank you, too, for the new trash bin. It's big enough that even the neighbor's Dalmatian can't tip it over."

How could he politely tell her he had no interest in small talk? Even though the two of them had never so much as shared an inappropriate glance when she'd been with Tom, the fact still weighed on Deacon that she'd been with him first. He couldn't have explained why, but when Tom had been alive, the former hookup hadn't been a big deal. Now it was.

"I'm, uh, glad to finally get a chance to talk." She sipped her white wine.

"Lord, Ell…" Head tipped back, Deacon released a long sigh. He couldn't do this. He could go days without sleep, food or shelter, but facing his best friend's widow? Wasn't happening. "I really don't have anything to say."

"That's fine." She nodded toward a more secluded area of the deck. "I'll do all the talking."

"What about Pia?"

"Ada's with her. Please, Deacon…."

He made the mistake of meeting Ellie's tear-filled gaze. Her blue eyes mesmerized, while at the same time made him feel like the world's biggest jackass for even thinking of skipping out on her, regardless of what she had to say.

"Why is it so hard for you to talk to me?"

"You know why." He glanced over his shoulder to ensure they weren't being overheard. "Last thing I want any of these people knowing is that I slept with the widow. Sure, it might've been before you met Tom, but it bugs me."

"You think the fact doesn't bother me? I'd give anything if we could take back that night, but we have to—"

"For whatever you feel you must say, now's not the time or place," he interrupted. "If it's waited this long, as far as I'm concerned, it can wait indefinitely."

Ellie was so shocked by Deacon's rejection, she couldn't react quickly enough to stop him from walking away. This was the second time that day he'd refused to talk to her. What was wrong with him? Was he missing a vital sensitivity gene?

Why ask? She already knew the answer. After their one wild night together, he hadn't invited her to spend the morning with him, or even asked for her number. He'd merely thanked her, before explaining he had a long-standing date with the gym.

Determined to once and for all get her most closely guarded secret off her chest, Ellie tried chasing after Deacon, but was cut off by the base commander and his wife.

"This has been such a great day," the portly, white-haired man said. "Paula and I think of Tom often."

"Thank you." Ellie was momentarily too consumed with her anger at Deacon to think straight, resulting in her blabbering the first thing to pop into her mind. "Tom thought highly of you. Just before he died, he quoted your Independence Day speech."

"Oh?"

Dabbing at tears with a tissue, she said, "He was playing with Pia when he reminded her, 'True bravery stems not necessarily from those with the biggest muscles, but the biggest hearts.'" Flashing a misty smile, Ellie added, "Only to him would that quote seem apropos, while purposely losing a game of tug-of-war with a baby."

The older man chuckled, and tears filled his wife's eyes.

"Where's Deacon?" Commander Duncan asked. "This anniversary must be hard on him, too."

"He, um, was here just a minute ago."

From the driveway came the muted, yet unmistakable revving of Deacon's Harley.

"Don't you worry, dear." Paula gave her husband's arm a reassuring squeeze. "We'll find him."

Good luck, since the weasel is at this very moment fleeing the premises.

ELLIE WAS BEYOND GRATEFUL for the day to finally be over. Tom's parents meant well, but remembering happier times in the presence of so many people had been harder than Ellie would've thought. Toss in her botched attempts to finally come clean with Deacon, and the afternoon had been an epic failure.

Out on the deck of her weathered, shingle-sided Cape Cod home, with a briny breeze drifting from the Atlantic, Ellie set the baby monitor on the side table, along with a freshly uncorked bottle of merlot. She'd long since lost the strappy heels that matched her floral sundress, and had freed her long, dark hair from the ponytail she'd resorted to while on the beach.

Tom had loved her hair down… Seated on his favorite lounge chair, the wine bottle resting between her breasts, she closed her eyes, imagining him there, leaning in close for a kiss, whispering how much he loved her and would always protect her and—

The pain balled in her chest was too much to bear.

Tears gushed, hot and stinging, until Ellie had difficulty breathing. This couldn't be happening. Even a year after the fact, she had a tough time believing her husband was really gone. The anniversary had dredged up too many painful memories. Of all their plans—not just for raising Pia, but projects for their home… Near the back picket fence, the one Tom had trained sweet pea vines to trail along, they'd talked about putting in a water garden. Ellie had wanted a trickling fountain. He'd wanted a train set that he could run with his angel, Pia.

Pia.

Such a huge burden her sweet baby unwittingly carried.

Tears started flowing again and Ellie upended the wine bottle, guzzling to find temporary relief where there was none. She dropped the bottle to the wood decking, and rolled onto her side, drawing her knees to her chest. She needed her husband so badly. With Tom gone, she didn't begin to know what to do. He'd completed her, and ever since his passing she'd felt empty and raw.

The French door opened and shut, startling Ellie. She glanced in that direction, only to have her heart sink. "What are you doing here?"

Deacon, still wearing the khakis and polo shirt he'd donned for the party, shrugged. "Wish I knew."

"Are you drunk?"

"Wishing for that, too, but…"

As much as she'd wanted to once and for all tell him everything, Ellie wasn't capable of dealing with him now. Not after the day she'd had.

"I was on the beach, thinking about all the shores I've been on with Tom, and somehow I ended up here." Hands in his pockets, Deacon shook his head. "I needed to be with someone who loved him like I do—*did*. Whatever. Tom was the greatest man I've ever known, and for the life of me, I can't figure why the big guy had him take that bullet instead of me. Literally six inches to the right and this would've all played out different. You'd be sitting here with him, shooting the breeze about me, and—"

"Stop," she begged, folding her arms tight. "You might've been with him when he died, but I was with him when he *lived*. I'd give anything if I could take back the night you and I shared. Most especially, I'd pray for Tom to be Pia's father instead of—" Clapping her hands to her mouth, she was thankful she'd stopped herself from confessing the secret she'd planned on delivering in a much saner way.

Deacon's dark eyes narrowed, his expression dangerous in the flickering light of a citronella candle. Ellie knew that, with a man as sharp as he was, she had already revealed too much.

"What are you saying?" he asked. "Tom wasn't Pia's dad?"

"Let it go, okay? We'll talk about it later." After grabbing the tipped wine bottle from the deck, Ellie stood, intending to go inside. She'd wanted to have this conversation earlier. The coward in her that had waited a whole year thought there'd be safety in revealing the truth in a more controlled setting.

"Then what did you mean?" He took her by her arm, spinning her to face him.

"Let me go," she said from between clenched teeth, struggling like a caged animal against the grip of a man who'd once given her the kind of hot, crazy, taboo sex she hadn't known existed outside of fiction. On that night, she might've been dazed with need for Deacon, but not now. Now, she knew him for the bad-boy, full-on disaster he was.

"Not until you come clean with me. She's mine, isn't she?" Releasing Ellie to run his hands over his face, he leaned against the deck rail.

She nodded.

"Wow..." He took the two steps down from the deck to pace the yard. "And Tom never knew?"

Hugging herself, tears falling in cold trails down her cheeks, Ellie shook her head.

"And that's what you wanted to tell me today? In front of everyone we know?" The look he cast her was indecipherable.

"If you don't mind," she replied, adopting an all-business tone, "I'd like to keep this between us. Helen and John will *always* be Pia's grandparents, but more and more, I'm seeing she needs a father. It's not fair for me to keep this from either of you."

Deacon sharply exhaled.

Arms crossed, he faced the sliver of glittering Atlantic visible from the yard. The view had been one of the things she and Tom loved most about the house.

What was Deacon thinking? Was he angry at her for not having told him sooner? She felt sick at how she'd handled everything.

"I owe you a massive apology," Ellie said, her voice small in the chilly breeze. "But from the second Tom learned I was pregnant, he was so happy. I couldn't take that from him—from myself. You know what kind of family I grew up in. I never wanted the same for my own child."

A sharp laugh escaped Deacon. "You're saying the right things, but all of a sudden, I don't even know you." Striding purposefully, he returned to the deck, only to open one of the French doors. Was he going to look in on his daughter?

"Please don't wake her." Ellie trailed behind him. "Pia's exhausted from playing. She needs her rest."

The dark look Deacon cast over his shoulder stoked

the firestorm in Ellie's stomach. "You drop this bomb on me, then not five minutes later have the nerve to dictate my every move?"

Chin raised, she said, "Forget everything you just heard. As far as I'm concerned, Pia's true father is dead."

Chapter Two

Deacon pushed his Harley to one-ten on his favorite lonely stretch of Shore Road before being forced to back down because of a tottering raccoon. Killing the engine, he climbed off, rolling his ride to the shoulder before dropping the kickstand to asphalt. At 3:00 a.m., he was pretty well guaranteed privacy until base commuters started pouring in.

After dropping his helmet to the seat, he ignored the burning behind his eyes and mounted the small dune standing between him and the angry Atlantic. What had been a soft breeze in town was now a wind whipping sand against his cheeks. Deacon liked it. Liked the pain.

One year ago today, it should've been him taking that bullet.

Aside from his SEAL team, he had no one in his life. His folks had long since written him off, and he couldn't say he blamed them.

Not bothering to remove his clothes or even his shoes, Deacon trudged into the surf, fighting his way out to black water, where the swells held him as surely as a lover. He generally saved this sort of thing for missions or triathalon training, but after tonight's chaos he needed the comfort found in the familiar. Out here, he knew where he stood. He'd been trained to handle any contingency with either sheer strength of will or ingenuity. What he wasn't equipped to deal with were his emotions.

What the hell was he supposed to do with this ache in his chest, making it so tight he feared it would explode? How did he look past images of his best friend dying in his arms, asking him to care for Ellie and his baby girl? Deacon had promised Tom he would, and he had, but he doubted his friend would have asked him if he'd known Deacon was the biological father of Tom's child.

With every stroke through black water, Deacon told himself it wasn't true, that Pia couldn't be his. But in his heart, he knew. Maybe he always had, but didn't want to admit it out of respect for the sanctity of his friendship with Tom. In certain areas, Deacon might not be the sharpest tool in the shed, but he'd always done great at remedial math. As much as he'd tried forgetting the things he and Ellie had done, the way she'd unwittingly made him so crazy to have her he hadn't even used a condom, the memories were still there, colliding with the respect he'd had for her husband. *His* best friend.

When Deacon's body finally got around to telling his brain he was hungry, cold and tired, he sliced his way to shore. He had to be on base by 0800—preferably with his head in some semblance of a good place.

"YOU REALLY DIDN'T NEED to come in this early," Ada declared, shortly after 9:00 a.m.

"Thanks," Ellie said, hugging her friend and boss. "But yes, I did. You're not going to believe what happened after you left."

"Not sure if I like the sound of this." As usual, Ada

looked runway ready, her makeup and hair flawlessly done. She'd retired from modeling to marry an NBA superstar, but when she caught him with a cheerleader, she'd been the last one laughing—at least from a financial perspective. The divorce settlement had afforded her the elegant boutique, where she designed several of the store's bestselling garments. "But you know me, always ready for a good story, especially if it's calorie free."

Having stashed her purse behind the counter, after leaving Pia at the part-time nursery school she loved, Ellie took the white leather armchair opposite her friend. "Deacon knows."

Ada covered her mouth with her hands. "Weren't you going to wait until the munchkin was a little bigger?"

"Yeah, well, I saw him yesterday and had a change of heart. Too many people told me his last mission was dicey. I couldn't live with myself if something happened to him and he never knew Pia was his. I tried telling him twice at the party, but both times got interrupted. Then what happens? He shows up at my house. One thing led to another, and instead of the calm, rational conversation I'd hoped for, I blurted it out."

"Whoa. Good thing we don't open till ten." Shifting in her chair, Ada asked, "What are you going to do?"

Ellie sighed. "I guess try to as smoothly as possible introduce Deacon into Pia's life. She already knows him, but not like a daughter should know her dad."

"Where do Helen and John fit in?"

"If Deacon has any respect for Pia or myself, he'll keep all of this on the down-low for at least a little longer. There's no way I'm ready for my in-laws to know. The news would crush them. They live for Pia."

"What about you? You're pretty attached to John and Helen, too."

"Granted. Last thing I want is for anything to rock that boat. Tom might be gone, but they're still my family."

"What about me?" Ada teased.

"Of course, you, too. But last I checked, I haven't given you just cause to disown me."

THAT NIGHT, after an endless day of firing drills, the last person Deacon wanted to find at his apartment door was Ellie, holding Pia in her arms.

Without so much as a hello, she asked, "You alone?"

"At least until Woof and Grinder get back with pizza and beer."

Behind her dark sunglasses, he imagined, she was rolling her eyes. More times than he could count, he remembered her voicing her dislike of grown men calling each other by nicknames. Woof happened to be Garrett Solomon, who had the uncanny knack of being able to puke like a dog one second, then be up on his feet, firing off rounds, the next. No physical discomfort fazed him. Grinder, aka Tristan Bartoni, had earned his name from downing six of the meaty Italian sandwiches in under ten minutes during their first leave from BUD/S training. The man ate more than any horse Deacon had ever met.

"We have to talk." Brushing past him, Ellie sat on the brown leather sofa. Since the three men were hardly ever in residence, the place was sparse, but held all necessary conveniences for a well-equipped man cave. Three recliners. Supersize, wall-mounted flat screen. Xbox, PlayStation and a fridge stocked with beer and the homemade boiled peanuts Southern boy Tristan had his mama send him each and every month. He'd once been married, but his wife couldn't handle his SEAL lifestyle and had bolted a few counties away with his son.

"If this is about last night," Deacon said, closing the door behind her, but preferring to stand rather than join her on the sofa, "I'm still processing, and this isn't a good time for hashing it all out."

"That's just it," she said with a brittle laugh. "There's nothing to *hash out*." She set Pia on the cushion beside her, only the kid promptly scooted off the sofa, making a beeline for Woof's brightly colored comic collection.

"Hey, whoa!" Deacon swooped to deter her. He hadn't meant to end up holding her, but now that he was, he took a good look. He and Tom had both been dark-haired, but Pia was a cotton top, much like Deacon's big brother, Peter, had been at that age. Her big brown eyes were like his, but Tom had also had the same shade. Ellie had hit the jackpot when it came to Baby Daddy Bingo. Had she not confessed that Pia belonged to Deacon, he'd never have been the wiser. He may have had questions, but considering he needed a kid about as much as he needed a hole in his head, he never would've asked. "Those comics aren't toys. Captain America set Uncle Woof back eight hundred big ones."

"Ridiculous," Ellie said under her breath. "All of you are hulking man-children with permission to use guns."

"And? You married one of our best." Deacon set Pia on her feet, pointing her in the opposite direction from his buddy's collection.

"Tom was different, and the jury's still out on what I feel for you." Ellie clenched her hands in her lap.

"Then why are you here? Because I'm not exactly feeling warm fuzzies for you." He wore desert camo fatigues with beige combat boots, the laces of which Pia tugged, then giggled.

"Up!"

He glanced down to find the toddler trying to climb his leg. Something about the stern set of determination in her jaw struck a familiar chord deep within him. Did she have his drive to succeed in whatever she started? But Tom had had the same drive. How was Deacon supposed to tell where his traits began and the ones she'd learned from Tom left off?

"She likes being held," Ellie said, leaving the couch to claim her daughter. "But you'll figure that out soon enough."

"Help me out here, Ell. You saying things like that lead me to believe you want me to have a relationship with Pia, yet I have to keep it a secret?"

"Exactly. You wouldn't blurt to Tom's parents that the two of us had a fling, would you?"

"No." Just thinking of that scenario had his pulse taking off. Which made him understand her reasoning behind the hush-hush attitude, though he couldn't say he liked it any better.

"More than anything, I think it's important that Pia know you as her father. But Tom's parents would be devastated to learn the truth, and I've still got enough of my own grief to deal with. I just can't…well, you know what I mean."

"Yeah." Deacon got the gist of her every word. He

might've inadvertently donated Pia's DNA, but when it came down to raising her, Ellie would appreciate him being MIA.

THE WHOLE RIDE HOME, Ellie couldn't stop trembling. Her relationship with Deacon—if it could even be called that—had always been tenuous at best. Since it had been Deacon who'd introduced her to Tom, she owed him an incalculable debt. But with Tom no longer with her, could that debt be considered paid in full? Technically, Deacon had also given her Pia, but with enough time, she'd have eventually been pregnant with Tom's child, right?

She didn't want to admit it, but Deacon scared her. With barely any effort, he'd released a side of her she hadn't even known existed. While their time together had been exhilarating, the aftermath had been somewhat terrifying. She was a good girl. She'd never been the type who would consider a one-night stand, let alone to engage in one without protection. Countless times she'd replayed the night in her mind, seeking answers. What had she been missing that a bad boy like Deacon filled?

From her car seat, Pia cooed, reminding Ellie that no matter how much she might personally wish to steer clear of Deacon, she couldn't deprive her daughter of knowing her father. Oddly enough, in having two fathers, Pia had been given a sort of do-over, in that if Ellie chose to let her, she could now begin a new life, with Deacon playing a starring role.

"Wooo!" cried the bosomy redhead Friday night when Deacon dipped her on the dance floor. "You're wild!"

"I do my best, darlin'." While the woman giggled as he twirled her to the honky-tonk song, he couldn't help but think of the time he'd held Ellie on this very spot. The fact that he could even remember such a thing was a sign he hadn't drunk nearly enough.

Four quick shots later and Deacon's head swam pleasantly.

It wasn't often a man commemorated the loss of his best friend, then learned he was the father of that friend's child, only to have said child snatched from him, all in the same week.

Worse yet, each time he touched the redhead's hips, in his mind's eye he saw Ellie naked and sprawled out before him, her blue eyes hazy with pleasure, her long inky hair playing hide and seek with her full breasts.

"Mind giving someone else a turn?" From behind him, a beer-bellied local copped an attitude. Ordinarily, Deacon would have graciously stepped aside, allowing a fellow dude the pleasure of a trip around the dance floor with a pretty lady. But as Deacon had already noted, there was nothing ordinary about this night, which was why he swung around to give the guy his best right.

"Hey, whoa!" Before he could launch another punch, Garrett grabbed Deacon's swinging arm, while Tristan took his left.

"Please forgive him," Tristan said to Deacon's victim, whose eye was already starting to bruise.

Garrett took the liberty of tugging Deacon's wallet from his back pocket and fishing out a few twenties. "Here," he said, handing them over as a peace offering. There was nothing Base Commander Duncan hated more than hearing one of his men had started trouble—

especially SEALs. "Our friend would love to buy your drinks for the rest of the night."

"The hell I would," Deacon snapped.

Tristan smacked the back of his head. "Would you shut up already?"

By the time his so-called friends shoved him into the backseat of Garrett's Mustang, Deacon needed another few shots. "I was all right back there. I hardly need you two finishing my fight."

"Yeah, yeah." Garrett made a sharp left that sent Deacon flying. "Put on your seat belt."

"Did he eat any of that pizza back at the apartment?" Tristan asked.

"Don't think so. Makes sense. He didn't eat lunch, either. Explains why he was such a lightweight."

"I'm right here," Deacon said to the two guys up front gossiping like old maids. "I hear everything you say."

Garrett asked Tristan, "He ever tell you why Ellie was driving away in tears as we showed up?"

"Nope. I was too hungry to ask."

Garrett nodded, glancing into the rearview mirror. "How about it? What was she even doing at our place?"

"I'll tell you," Deacon said, "but then I'll have to kill you."

"Fair enough." Tristan angled to face him. "What'd you say that had her so upset and you drunker than I've seen you since finishing hell week?"

"You know Pia?" Deacon asked. "Tom and Ellie's baby girl?"

"Well, yeah." Stopped at a red light, Garrett glanced in the mirror. "She all right?"

"Oh—" Deacon had to laugh "—she's just hunky-dory. Especially since I'm supposed to be her dad, only not around Tom's folks."

"What?" Garrett had just accelerated from zero to sixty, only to slam on the brakes, fishtailing into an empty grocery store lot. "Please tell me you didn't just claim to be the father of your dead best friend's kid."

"WHAT DO YOU MEAN, he's not here?" Ellie felt bad enough about her last conversation with Deacon that guilt had driven her to ask Helen to watch Pia so Ellie could find him on base. She'd failed to tell Helen the true nature of her urgent errand.

The base security officer checked a computer screen. "I'm sorry, Mrs. Hilliard, but Chief Petty Officer Murphy isn't available."

"He should be. Do you know where his team is?"

"Mrs. Hilliard, you know I'm not allowed to disclose that information."

It took every shred of Ellie's patience to thank the man and make an unhurried U-turn in the space so thoughtfully provided.

Damn the navy. Double damn all SEALs.

How many times had she needed Tom, only to be told he was unavailable? And then he'd show up days later, unable to tell her where or why he'd been gone. As much as she'd loved him, that portion of their relationship had been unnerving. All the pretty Virginia Beach barflies dreamed of snagging a SEAL. Little did they know that even after closing the deal, their lives would never be perfection. As much as she'd loved Tom, she'd equally missed him.

Where was Deacon?

Was he as upset as she was about the way they'd left

things? Of course she wanted him to be Pia's father in every sense of the word; she just wasn't ready for Helen and John to know. Not yet. Deacon had to understand.

Why? a tiny voice prodded. *Pia is his daughter.* A flesh and blood part of him. Once Deacon got over the initial shock of learning he was a father, he would never back down. Not until the whole world knew Pia was his. Unfortunately for Ellie, he morally and legally had that right.

"I STILL CAN'T BELIEVE you just walked away."

"From what?" At 1930 hours, Deacon glanced across the belly of the C-130 transport hauling them south to the Congo, where a U.S. ambassador and his family were being held for ransom by representatives of the wannabe government du jour.

From on top of an equipment crate, Garrett popped a sunflower seed in his mouth, snapping the shell open with his teeth. "Your daughter."

"Stay out of it," Deacon warned, his head still throbbing from his earlier activities at the bar. He had to cut back. Last thing he felt like doing was shouting above engine noise.

"No, seriously. You know what Tristan's been through, missing his son. He tries hiding it with partying, but you don't wanna end up hurting like him." Garrett tucked the sunflower hull into his already bulging shirt pocket before grabbing another seed, then hopping down to join Deacon on one of the few rows of seats installed for their journey. "I never told you this, but I had a kid."

One eye open, Deacon snorted. "You're full of crap."

"For real. Knocked up my high school sweetheart.

Her dad shipped her off to some girls' home, where she had my son, but he died."

Deacon straightened. "Sorry, man. That's awful."

Shrugging, Garrett said, "It's not anything I advertise."

"Still…" Funny, how all of SEAL Team 12 had been through hell and back together, but there were still things Deacon didn't know about his friends. With the remainder of their team either sleeping or off playing cards, he had the privacy to ask, "How did you work through something like that? Even a year later, losing Tom is damn near killing me. I can't imagine losing a kid."

"Compartmentalization, baby." Tapping the side of his head, Garrett said, "Anything in me stings, I stick it in a box and shove it in the mental attic. Every so often—say, at Christmas—I take it out, toy with it a little—you know, wonder how different my life might be had our son lived. Would I have ended up with the girl? Ever joined the navy? Who knows?" He shrugged. "All I'm saying is that Pia is very much alive and cute as a bug. You should make getting to know her a priority."

"Okay, whoa." Deacon shook his head. "It's hardly that simple. Ellie was Tom's woman, not mine. The fact that she had my kid and not his is a crazy twist of fate. If guilt hadn't been eating her alive over the fact that Pia needs a father and still has one, I don't think she'd ever have told me I'm that guy. I know for a fact, now she did, that she wishes she hadn't. She told me to my face she doesn't want anyone—especially Tom's folks—learning the truth."

"Doesn't matter." Garrett popped another seed. "Way I see it, now that the cat's out of the bag, you gotta feed it. Let's say Tom was still alive when this came out. He knew you and Ellie had a fling."

"He did?" Deacon sat up so abruptly he nearly choked on his spit.

"*Everyone* did. Thing is, he loved you like a brother, man. What happened with you and Ellie was in the past. He staked claim to her future. He never said anything, but given the short timing between their marriage and Pia's birth, even he had to wonder. I know me and Tristan did."

Deacon winced.

"Just think about it—becoming that little girl's dad. She's missing Tom, too. Maybe you could work through it together?"

AFTER TUMBLING FROM the plane's belly in the dead of night, then floating silently to hostile ground, Deacon now stood, M-16 at the ready, just outside the U.S. ambassador's home. The team stayed in the shadows—not easy, considering the obscene level of exterior lighting. They were used to trekking through desolate jungle or desert for miles to reach their targeted engagement arena, but this time had been different. Dropped on the outskirts of the capital city, they'd used lush tropical vegetation to their advantage.

The place was your typical British colonial, two-story mansion, complete with a glowing turquoise pool. The lower level featured plenty of open living space, which no doubt had contributed to the ease with which the bad guys had helped themselves to the ambassador and his family.

Aside from crickets, the only sound was tango music

playing softly through hidden speakers. Above that rose an infant's cries.

Once the team had surrounded the home, eliminating the remaining guards in the process, their leader gestured Deacon, Garrett and two other team members inside for a sweep. One by one, they searched the elegant rooms—now trashed—until on the second floor, they found a preteen male zip-tied to a desk chair, his mouth covered with duct tape. Given his wild eyes and dirty tearstained cheeks, Deacon wasn't sure his immediate release was a great idea.

The spooked kid appeared capable of making a lot of noise.

On the other hand, he could also let them in on the secret of why the place felt voodoo deserted.

Deacon locked gazes with the kid, then put his finger to his mouth to urge him to silence.

Okay? Deacon hand-gestured to see if he understood.

The boy nodded.

The infant kept crying.

Deacon nodded to Garrett, who used his knife to eliminate the youth's restraints.

Arms free, the kid removed the tape from his mouth. He whispered, "I don't know where my parents are, but my baby sister's still in her nursery."

Deacon pointed to a closet, motioning for the kid to enter it. "We'll come back for you. Until then, don't move."

Garrett led them out of the room, back to the wide, wood-floored hall. Someone had targeted a vase filled with fresh flowers on a marble-topped table and shot it to hell. A sick confetti of tropical greenery and blooms littered the water-slick planks.

Room after room they found ransacked and void of life.

The infant's ever-increasing wails grew harder to bear, but for fear they were walking into a trap, they couldn't break the protocol of slowly securing the entire area.

Finally, Deacon and Garrett reached what must've once been a pretty nursery, only to now find *"Die America"* written in what appeared to be blood on yellow floral wallpaper.

Peering over the edge of a dark wood crib, Deacon found the source of the tears, only to recoil in horror. The infant wearing soiled pink pajamas couldn't have been much over six months old. She also happened to sport a belt comprised of neat white strips of C-4 explosives attached to a blasting cap and timer. The glowing red digital display read :32, then clicked to :31, :30…

"Damn!" Deacon took what knowledge he had of the explosive to rationalize that without the blasting cap, the C-4 was stable. The problem was figuring which plastic-coated line was attached to what.

Outside, gunfire erupted.

The automatic rounds could be heard pinging off the house's plaster exterior.

:20…

:19…

"Smile," Garrett said, nodding toward a cheap video cam someone had thoughtfully set on a dresser. "We're on *Candid Camera*."

"Damn." With twelve seconds to go, sweat literally dripped from Deacon's forehead onto the wires he needed to clip. Odds were, whoever had planned this show wasn't smart enough to have booby-trapped the

explosives. Regardless, it was too late to do anything about it now.

At seven seconds, he said a prayer and eased his knife between rows of what looked like pale sticks of butter, to have his eye catch on what earlier had blended in. Velcro. The entire bloody thing was attached to the infant with simple strands of Velcro.

At four seconds, he ripped open the closure.

At three seconds, he kicked out the window.

Chapter Three

Ellie sipped green tea, staring out rain-streaked windows to the dark yard. How many times had she performed this vigil for Tom? Wondering where he was. What he was doing. Now that he was gone, she should've felt at peace, knowing he was safe in the arms of angels. But with Deacon now in danger, along with all Tom's other team members, apprehension was still Ellie's closest companion.

Wind shook the small house, pelting rain so hard against the glass it sounded like tacks hitting the panes. The night was miserable, blustery and colder than normal for the end of summer.

Though exhaustion clung to her like a heavy sheet, dulling her senses, sleep was out of the question. Ellie had tried reading, but her thoughts were too frenetic. TV held no appeal.

Wandering into the nursery, she peered at her child, at the long lashes sweeping those chubby cheeks. Even at rest, Pia's beauty never failed to thrill her. Ellie and Tom had had epic, laughing battles over what their little girl might grow to be. Tom had claimed Pia was destined to be the first female SEAL. Ellie had insisted she would for sure be a doctor or movie star—maybe both.

Was Tom looking down on them now? If so, what did he think of Ellie's deception? Would he have hated her for not telling the truth from the start? Or understood and appreciated her rationale, and invited Deacon to be an integral part of Pia's life?

Setting her tea on a nearby bookshelf, Ellie covered her stinging eyes with the heels of her hands. Given the chance to do it all over, would she wish her night with Deacon had never happened?

One look at her child confirmed what she already knew—that no matter who Pia's father was, Ellie loved her with every breath in her body. The night she and Deacon shared had given her life's ultimate gift. By introducing her to Tom, Deacon had given her yet another present of incalculable worth.

Were he here, she would thank him.

But only after begging him to maintain her small family's status quo.

WHEN THE TIMER HIT two seconds, Deacon tossed the C-4 explosive out the hole where there had once been a window.

At one second, he cradled the baby against him while the whole house rattled violently from concussive force.

Deacon held tight to the now-screaming baby girl. Even from outside, the fire's heat could be felt.

"Nicely done," Garrett shouted. "But we gotta get out of here." Rounds of gunfire could now be heard above the roaring flames.

"No kidding."

Garrett radioed that they'd accomplished their mission of scouting the house and securing remaining occupants.

With insurgents outside, apparently pissed to have had their big, televised show of force to the Western world ruined, Deacon led the way at a hurried, albeit cautious pace down the hall toward the boy.

They found him still in the closet, cowering in a corner with his hands over his head.

"Come on," Deacon shouted, "your sister's safe. Let's get you out of here."

"B-but they're shooting."

"I know," Deacon said above the noise, "but would you rather die from fire or a bullet?"

"I don't wanna die!" the kid wailed.

"Me neither," Deacon cried. "Which is why we've gotta haul ass to somewhere safe. Come on! Pretend we're in a video game!"

Garrett helped the kid to his feet, and a minute later, keeping to back staircases, they slipped into a basement and crawled out a window that led to a formal garden. The visual serenity of dimly lit, winding gravel paths among fragrant flowers felt incongruous given the gunfire surrounding them. The baby let them all share her discomfort with continued screams.

A minute later, the firing stopped.

Through his earpiece, Deacon's commander said, "Cease fire. Rendezvous like ghosts at staging area five."

Garrett snorted. "Easy for him to say. He doesn't have a screaming baby in tow."

"How do I get her quiet?" Deacon asked the girl's brother.

"She's probably scared and hungry, and needs her diaper changed."

Right. None of those bases had been adequately covered in training.

By now, local officials were arriving, sirens blaring, red and blue lights adding to the already chaotic scene. It would be simple enough to run around front and ask for medical assistance. Trouble was, not knowing which government was currently in charge, or their opinion of the good old U.S.A., put them in a bind.

As Deacon's commander had said, they needed to be ghosts, leaving as stealthily as they'd arrived.

With the staging area a good mile east, Deacon cradled the infant as close to his chest as he could while still hugging shadows and staying alert for additional danger. Most of all, he prayed his own daughter never found herself in this much danger.

FIVE DAYS AFTER Ellie had last spoken to Deacon, she opened the front door to him, the scent of honeysuckle heavy in the twilight's warmth. Knees rubbery, she had to keep a strong hold on the door frame so as not to crumple.

"Hey." He was dressed in cargo shorts and a navy T-shirt. Even with his eyes hidden by gold-rimmed Ray-Bans, Deacon looked exhausted, but still steal-your-breath handsome. Tall, with broad shoulders and a square jaw sporting stubble. His dark hair had grown out of its usual buzz and now was a rummaged-through mess. When he smiled—oh, when he smiled—that was when she'd always had to work to keep her pulse from racing. White teeth and a lopsided dimple drew in the ladies more effectively than a 75% off sale at Jimmy Choo.

"I'd ask where you've been," she quipped, striving

for a lighthearted tone, beyond relieved that he was okay, "but Tom taught me better."

"Yeah, uh…" With a bottle of Patrón in hand, he brushed past her. When their shoulders touched, her throat knotted from the unexpected pleasure of sharing his warmth. Impossible to explain, but she felt an irrational connection to him. "Sorry for the abrupt exit. You know how it is," he murmured.

She did. And in many ways, being a SEAL's wife had sucked.

Nodding to ward off tears ready to spill, she said, "I'm having iced tea. Want a glass?"

"Thanks, but—" he waved his unopened bottle "—I brought my own refreshment."

While Ellie bustled into the kitchen to refill her glass, Deacon stood on the threshold, hands crammed in his pockets. Did he, too, feel awkward about the way their last conversation had ended?

From over the baby monitor, Pia let loose a few fitful whines. She'd crashed earlier than usual tonight. Striving for some semblance of normalcy, Ellie had taken her to their weekly play group comprised of base moms and toddlers. Ellie had hoped it'd be fun, but with her naval husband gone, more and more she felt she no longer belonged. Everyone was still kind, but Ellie found they had less and less in common.

"Be right back." She nodded toward the nursery.

Deacon blocked her path. "Let me."

"No. You're holding booze."

"*Holding.* Not drinking."

She wanted to deny him, but the hard set of his jaw told her he wasn't backing down.

For a good five minutes, she watched him from the

edge of the sofa that allowed her a view into her daughter's room. Pia had long since quieted and now Deacon just sat there, elbows on his knees, chin on his fists, staring. As if in a trance, he was stone still. The bottle of Patrón never left the floor.

Was his behavior a result of the mission he'd just completed, or more? Had he only just now absorbed the gravity of becoming a father? If so, what did that mean for her? For Pia?

Unable to bear the current scene, Ellie brewed coffee. Not for her, but for Deacon. He took it black.

Strange how she knew dozens of mundane facts about him, ranging from his coffee preferences to his aversion to broccoli. She'd known him intimately, yet for all practical purposes, they were strangers. Strangers who shared a child.

An hour passed.

Ellie folded laundry, dusted the contents of her curio cabinet, unloaded the dishwasher, stared at the paperwork necessary for volunteering at a local alcoholic outreach program. Ada thought helping others might get Ellie's mind off her own worries, but Ellie wasn't so sure.

Finally, without a sound other than leather flip-flops hitting his heels, Deacon went out onto the deck, tequila in hand. He didn't bother to shut the door. Temperature-wise, it was pleasant outside, but the breeze came from just the right direction to ease under the seascape hanging behind the sofa, making it clap against the wall.

After pouring Deacon a mug of his favorite Kona blend, she joined him outside. Baby monitor in hand, she shut the door behind her.

Deacon stood at the rail, staring into the night.

"Thanks," he said when she handed him the mug.

"You're welcome. Want to sit down?"

Though he shrugged, as if on autopilot, he crossed the short distance to the table with its comfy, red-cushioned chairs. He hadn't removed his sunglasses. Meaning she still had no clue as to what he was thinking.

"Nice night, huh?" Ellie's stab at conversation seemed to fall on deaf ears.

Deacon had zeroed in on his bottle. He drank his coffee down to half-full, then eyed the tequila. "She's really something," he said, more to himself than to Ellie. "Pia, I mean. Before…well, I never really noticed."

"You were over here all the time, Deacon. It wasn't like Tom and I put her in the cupboard when you barged in for a free meal."

He half laughed. "It was different then. Pia belonged to Tom."

And now she's yours.

The elephant in the room between them. Only they weren't in a room, and she wasn't in any position to give parental advice.

Deacon cleared his throat. "I saw some crazy shit the past few days."

"Language," she scolded.

"Right." He downed more coffee. "Sorry."

"It's okay. Even though Pia isn't out here now, it's good to get in the habit of not cursing. I was constantly reminding Tom we had a little sponge just waiting to one day arrive in kindergarten not knowing her ABCs, but fluent in every SEAL curse."

"Kindergarten. Wow." Deacon shook his head. "Yeah, that wouldn't be good."

Fat, endless minutes of silence passed, with nothing between them but the rush of wind in the trees.

Finally, Deacon said, "We both know why I'm here, so let's stop pussyfooting around."

Ellie wasn't sure what he meant. Did she even want to know? she wondered, her mouth dry.

"Without letting you in on any state secrets, I just witnessed some shi—stuff—that blew my mind. In my years of service, I've seen a lot, but this…" He shook his head. "Before he died, Tom, uh—" Deacon glanced away. "He, um, asked me to look after you and Pia." Turning back to Ellie, he slipped off his sunglasses and set them on the table. Even in the shadowy light leaking from the house, his eyes looked horrible. Bloodshot. His right cheek sported a bruise. It took everything in her not to gasp.

What happened to you? "Wh-what else did Tom say?" And why was this the first time Deacon had brought it up?

"That's pretty much it, aside from asking me to tell you and his folks how much he loved them. I—I guess with this anniversary, I've been so caught up in how I'm feeling, I forgot I'm not the only one missing him. Tom was a good guy. The best."

"I know." Ellie didn't even try holding back her silent tears.

"He deserved to be Pia's dad."

Ellie nodded, relief streaming through her.

Obviously, whatever Deacon had gone through had showed him how important it was for Pia to have continuity in her life. Yes, Ellie was all for Deacon playing an important role in her daughter's upbringing—like that of a favorite uncle. No one would have to know he was actually the girl's biological father.

"That said—" Deacon clasped his hands on the table, locking their gazes "—with Tom out of the picture, Garrett helped me see that she's going to need her real father more than ever."

Straightening in her chair, Ellie shook her head. "You told Garrett what was supposed to have been our secret?"

"Tristan, too. But he's cool. They're both like family."

Pressing her hands to her superheated face, Ellie wasn't sure whether to laugh or cry. "Those two blunderheads you call Woof and Grinder are hardly my family. Sure, you all might've worked together, but that doesn't mean beans."

"You need to hush before I get angry. Lucky for you, your husband was a SEAL. We take care of our own. You don't have a clue what it takes to become a SEAL, which means you don't know jack about how hard we'll fight for what we love. I loved Tom more than I cared for my own brother. Because of that, you and Pia are under my protection. Admittedly, I'm off to a rocky start, but during the heat of what I just went through—unwrapping C-4 from a baby's belly—I vowed to never let anything near that kind of horror befall my baby girl."

Mouth dry, Ellie stammered, "Wh-what does that mean?"

"It means I need to try being a father. We both know I'm going to make mistakes, but at least I'll be there for her, right?"

"I don't understand."

"We live in a scary freaking world. What kind of

man would I be, letting my own kid grow up without protection?"

"Um, right…" Deacon didn't know the first thing about being a father. His speech was all "rah, rah, I'm a SEAL, hear me roar" B.S. "But you plan on doing all of this without the rest of the world knowing, right? You'll essentially be a private parenting partner?"

Palms flat against the table, he laughed. "Seriously? Are we back to your worries over Tom's parents finding out you're an adult woman who dared have an adult dalliance before you even met their son?"

"What's wrong with you?" Ellie said in a whispered hiss. "My husband's barely been a year in his grave. His family and Pia are the only things keeping me sane. How dare you step foot in my home and make demands?"

"That's you putting your own spin on my words. I've been trained to handle situations, and we certainly have a doozy here. Bottom line, I'm Pia's father, and as such, I'm more than ready to step up to the parenting plate. If you need more time to adjust to my taking on this role in a formal capacity—" he shrugged "—I guess I can live with that. But not for long."

When relief over the fact that Deacon wasn't dead set on rushing to John and Helen first thing in the morning flowed through her, Ellie sharply exhaled. She also released the iron grip she'd held on her emotions. All at once, fear and grief and anger for even getting herself in this position poured from her in ugly tears.

"Hey, whoa…" In true Deacon style, he stood up and backed away.

"Please, just go," Ellie said, swiping at her cheeks. Instead of doing as she asked, he shocked her by pausing, then taking a few awkward steps forward and drawing her into a loose, equally awkward hug. She wanted to push him away, convinced she didn't need his pity. But it turned out she did. With grief rising in her belly, threatening to cut off all air, she clung to him, fisting his shirt, resting her head against his warm, solid chest.

He tightened his hold, burying his face in her hair. "It's okay. Let it out."

"I—I can't. I—I have to stay strong for Pia. And Tom's parents."

"I'm here. Lean on me."

She did, crying until the only tears remaining were the ones deep inside she feared would haunt her for years to come.

When she finally felt strong enough to stand on her own, she drew back, intending to thank Deacon for being there. Only his eyes were misty, too.

"Of all the people in the world," she said hoarsely, "you and I were the only ones who really, truly knew him. His parents loved him, but they didn't know him. Not like we did."

Deacon nodded.

"I've wanted to tell you about Pia for a long time now, but the timing never felt right."

"It's okay…" He shook his head. "Well, it's not okay that you kept this from me, but now that I know, I deserve the chance to prove I can be a good man. Never in Tom's league, but for Pia's sake, at least close."

"But you're not pushing the whole official daddy title, right?"

Tipping his head back, Deacon groaned. "You're like a dog with a bone. Leave it alone, Ell. Like it or not, as

Garrett says, I *am* Pia's father. I'm trying to be sensitive here. Really, I am. But there's only so much a guy can stand." He gave her a glare before turning to look out to sea. "I'm good enough for you to cry on, but not for anyone to know I fathered your kid?"

As if wanting to say more, but holding back, he laughed before reaching for his Patrón. He walked down the steps off the deck and stood at the back fence. Ellie watched as he tipped up the bottle repeatedly.

She should've gone to him, but couldn't.

The most she could manage was taking and hiding his motorcycle key.

And just when she'd thought all her tears had been spent, they returned with a vengeance. Were it not for her fears of Tom's parents learning she wasn't the perfect wife they'd imagined her to be, Deacon would still be sober beside her, making her world a less lonely place.

Why couldn't he understand how much was at stake if she admitted Tom hadn't been Pia's dad?

Why can't you understand Deacon has every right in the world to share the truth whenever and with whomever he pleases?

Chapter Four

The morning sun was like a laser in his eyes when Deacon woke on Ellie's sofa, feeling as if he'd been kicked by the mule he'd encountered in a rural area on his last mission. Worse yet, from the nursery, Pia wailed. Where was Ellie?

The restroom needed to be first on his priority list, but his mission to the Congo had left zero tolerance for baby tears, so he headed straight for the nursery.

He scooped Pia from her crib. "Hey."

Huffing, red-eyed and offended, she stared at him, harder than any woman he'd ever wronged.

"Ouch." Leave it to a female to make him feel even worse, when for once he was trying to do the right thing.

Ellie's bedroom door was closed.

He found the baby monitor off and sitting on the kitchen counter. Assuming Ellie needed the rest if she had been tired enough to forget it, he set Pia in an armchair. "Stay. I've really got to take care of business."

Back from the bathroom, Deacon found his daughter off the chair and making a beeline for a giant potted fern.

"Whoa…" Snatching her around her waist, he held her gaze with his. "Since when are you such a rebel?"

She blew a raspberry.

"And you stink."

Her giggle didn't do much to alleviate the smell.

In his role as Uncle Deacon, he hadn't done much in the way of Pia's care. Meaning when it came to changing a diaper, he didn't know squat. How hard could it be?

In the nursery, he started the mission much as any other, by gathering supplies. Clean diaper—check. Wipes. Powder. Lotion. Fresh snappy pajama-thingee.

He figured the table sporting a raised edge and floral pad on top was for changing, and he set Pia there. Only all the supplies were on the counter section of the built-in cabinets and bookshelf.

Eyeing his daughter, he asked, "If I leave you here, are you going to stay?"

The gleam in her eyes told him he'd asked a stupid question. The monkey would be gone faster than he could call her name.

It took a couple trips, but he finally had the equipment and the child in the same place. Unsnapping her PJs was simple enough, but they were damp, so he wrestled them off, being careful with her arms, as they struck him as somewhat floppy. Normal? He didn't have a clue.

The dirty diaper was problematic.

Sticky tabs had been made with a super polymer resin apparently tough enough to withstand Pia and others of her kind, yet not especially user friendly for those in a caretaking position. Wishing for his Bowie knife, he settled for ripping, which made for a whole new problem. The fluffy stuff inside the diaper that held the pee? Not cool.

Deacon had wiped, lotioned and powdered when Pia decided to pee again. "Seriously?"

Lucky for her, she already had a killer smile.

Repeating the whole process, adding the diaper, then gently cramming her gangly limbs into ridiculously small clothing holes finally netted him a pleasant-smelling kid. The snaps were out of order, but those were way over his head in level of difficulty.

"Good Lord," Deacon mumbled on his way back to the kitchen, holding Pia on his right hip. "That was too intense for this early in the day. Know where Mommy keeps her aspirin?"

"Mommy!" Pia's smile faded and she was back to making the huffy noises she'd produced when he'd first wrangled her from her crib.

Deacon found headache relief in the cabinet alongside the fridge, then poured himself OJ. "Want some?"

He held the juice glass to Pia's mouth, but she made a sour face.

Checking the fridge, he found bacon and eggs. Nothing took care of a hangover like a big breakfast. "You're gonna like my bacon, Miss Pia. Back when me and your dad shared a place, he said I didn't cook it long enough—actually told me the pig was still oinking. But I told him to—well, never mind what I said. Probably not anything fit for your tender ears."

Deacon found a frying pan and started enough bacon cooking for Ellie to have some, too. He wasn't sure what the munchkin ate. Only knew that as long as he kept talking, she didn't cry. Using goofball accents even earned him the occasional giggle.

"What are you doing?" As she marched toward him, wearing black booty shorts and a pink tank top, Ellie's scowl matched her daughter's. "You can't hold her next to the stove. What if the bacon splatters?"

"Good point," Deacon said, while Ellie snatched Pia from his arms. "Rookie mistake I hadn't considered."

"A mistake that could land her in the emergency room."

"Whoa!" He held up his hands. "Lesson learned. Just trying to help out."

"Well, when she woke up, I wish you had come get me."

Clenching his jaw, Deacon summoned every ounce of what bit of gentleman remained in him to not let Ellie have it. What was her problem? If she hadn't left Pia's monitor in the kitchen, he might still be sleeping. Granted, he shouldn't have had Pia near the stove. It'd been a mistake, but nothing worthy of this attack.

After turning off the burner, he dumped the bacon on a plate then tossed the pan in the sink. "Where are my keys?"

She took them from a teacup in her curio cabinet. "Here."

"Not sure what your issue is—" he bounced the keys in his palm "—but you need to get over it. I was only trying to help."

Deacon left.

When the sound of his motorcycle's powerful engine faded, and the only proof he'd been there was the acrid smell of exhaust drifting through the open kitchen window, Ellie finally allowed herself to exhale.

"What just happened?" she asked her child, wishing she was old enough to hold an intelligent conversation. But then that would open an entirely new box of issues. When Pia was five or ten or eighteen, what would she think about her mother wanting to hide the fact that Deacon was her real father?

Setting Pia in her high chair, fixing her oatmeal with raisins, and filling her sippy cup with apple juice side-tracked Ellie's racing mind for a few minutes. But that was only a temporary fix.

She feared what had upset her most about finding Deacon holding her daughter—*their* daughter—had little to do with lethal bacon grease and more to do with the fact that her baby girl had been happy. Grinning in her father's arms. Though Ellie had known it was past time for Deacon to learn the truth, she'd been naive to assume he'd have no problem hiding the fact that he was a parent. Her carefully balanced pile of secrets was poised to topple, and as much as the thought terrified her, she realized that for Pia's sake—and Deacon's—full disclosure was for the best. A girl needed her father.

Even if, in the process, the fallout destroyed her mother.

"I WAS SO NOT IN THE MOOD for this." Deacon set his rebreather unit on the aft end of the Mark V Special Operations Craft. Breathing pure oxygen for hours at a time when he'd started his morning with a killer headache had only made his day worse.

"Come on," Garrett teased, with an elbow to Deacon's ribs. "How can you not love practicing for disarming nukes at three hundred feet?" Unzipping his dry suit, he tilted his head back to take in the sun. "It's the dark that gets me. The black swallows you whole."

"Yeah." Deacon began the long process of disassembling and stowing his gear. They would rinse off the seawater back on base.

Garrett joined in the mundane task, asking, "What's up with you? You've been off all day—I mean, beyond your hangover."

"Remember our last conversation about Pia?" Deacon checked to make sure none of the rest of their team were within eavesdropping distance.

"Sure. You take my advice and see her?"

Deacon winced. "Yes and no."

Groaning, Garrett said, "Man, you've got to lay off the sauce—especially around your kid."

"It wasn't like that." Deacon bristled. "I wasn't going to drink at all, but then Ellie made me crazy. One thing led to another and somehow I downed the better half of a bottle. Ellie took my keys and I passed out on her sofa."

"This just keeps getting better...." Garrett shook salt water from his fins.

"So this morning, I hear Pia crying. Wanting to try my hand at the whole responsible dad thing, I handled it. Got the kid scrubbed down, and I would've fed her, too, but Ellie flipped. I'm cooking bacon, with Pia in my arms, and she practically accuses me of child abuse. Says I'm gonna burn her with grease. The whole scene was nuts."

Garrett didn't answer, just kept messing with his gear.

"What? You think I was in the wrong?"

"No. Just put yourself in Ellie's shoes. Not only did she lose her husband, but now she's got this deep dark secret threatening to spill. Tom's folks think the world of her and Pia. They're her support system. What happens if she loses them, too?"

"Hadn't considered that." Sitting back on his heels,

Deacon strove to balance himself against the Mark V's 45-knots-per-hour bounce. "But you told me I should take an active role in raising my kid. Now you're saying, for Ellie's sake, I shouldn't?"

"Not at all. For Pia's sake, for sure you should. Just maybe take it a little slower. No more passing out on the couch, for one. And two, put the baby in her high chair before handling popping grease."

"EVERYTHING'S PERFECT." Tom's mother, Helen, used a pushpin to add a pink balloon to the last pink streamer. "I doubt Pia will remember any of this, but I'm in desperate need of cheer. My granddaughter's second birthday couldn't be a more perfect excuse."

"Agreed." Ellie dropped raspberry sherbet into a bowl of pink lemonade punch. It had been a month since she'd seen Deacon, who'd been off on another mission. It'd been over a year since Tom's passing. Every day she hoped missing him would get easier, but if anything, the fact that he really wasn't coming back was sinking in. The heartbreaking finality of his absence, in everything from deciding whether or not to repair the broken washer or buy a new one, to what to have for Sunday supper, was taking an emotional toll.

Ellie's only bright spot was Pia. She talked more every day and now had a working vocabulary of about thirty words—mostly commands for what she wanted Ellie to do. *Play, hot, cold, food, ouch.* How badly Ellie wanted to share these milestones with Tom. How guilt-ridden she was for not sharing them with Deacon.

She'd invited him to Pia's big day, but in the same breath prayed he'd stay away.

"These are delicious." Tom's father helped himself to

a cherry cupcake with cream cheese icing. "Ellie, you sure know how to cook."

"Thanks." She glowed at the man's kind words. Her home life had been far from idyllic, growing up, which made her cherish her relationship with Helen and John all the more. "It's a new recipe, so I'm relieved they turned out."

Guests started arriving.

Ada. Neighbors. Friends from her old Mommy and Me crowd, as well as her widow support group and new alcoholic outreach program. She'd recently begun working with Pandora, a young alcoholic mother who'd lost her child to foster care. Though Ellie hadn't admitted it to Ada, the work was extremely satisfying, going a long way toward making Ellie finally recognize she wasn't a helpless little girl anymore. Bad things might occasionally happen in her life, but she was ultimately in control of how she reacted to those events. The more friends who arrived, the more relieved Ellie felt that Deacon wasn't among them.

Helen turned on a kid-friendly CD and soon the normally serene backyard was transformed into a riot of frosting-smudged kids running wild on sugar and fun.

Ellie was at the kitchen counter making a fresh batch of punch when the back door swung open.

"Where's the birthday girl?" In walked Deacon, brandishing a huge beribboned box. "Sorry I'm late. Pia's gift was a special-order thing, and it just came in this morning."

Ellie's hands were trembling so badly she dropped the last scoop of sherbet down the garbage disposal. She tried finding words, but none made it past her dry mouth. He wore jeans and an untucked cobalt button-down that, when he removed his sunglasses, did the most amazing thing to his brown eyes. The man wasn't just handsome, he was breathtaking—and he knew it.

Wielding his smile as if they'd seen each other just the other day, he asked, "Anyplace special you have assigned for presents?"

"I, um…" She wiped her sticky fingers on a dishrag. "Just put it anywhere. I didn't think you were coming."

"Why wouldn't I?" he asked with an extra helping of charm. "I'm Pia's father."

"Who hasn't seen her in a month."

"Through no fault of my own." There he went again with his smile. "You can thank Afghan rebels for my absence, but I'm here now and psyched."

"You could've let me know you've been on a mission. I had to find out through friends."

"Sorry," he said, still smiling. "You know how it is. After our last talk, I assumed you'd understand that would be the only reason I wouldn't show up. Regardless, forgive me?"

What a loaded question. On one hand, there was nothing to forgive him for. On the other, she wanted to blame him for being Pia's father. But how could she when she'd played an equal role in the utterly careless abandon that fatal night? Moreover, her daughter was her world—more than ever since Ellie had lost Tom. If anything, in some twisted way, she owed Deacon great thanks for wanting to tackle this most important job with his usual SEAL drive to excel.

"Of course I forgive you. But you have to do the same for me. I didn't mean to come down so hard on you about the bacon. I just…" Hands to her forehead, she searched for an explanation for the chaos in her heart that had stemmed from seeing Pia in his arms. "Well, not that it's an excuse, but with the anniversary of Tom's death, and telling you about Pia, I was having a rough time."

"Ellie, are there more—" Helen saved her by arriving in the kitchen with an empty cupcake platter. "Deacon!"

When she drew him into a hug, Ellie fought an irrational jealous twinge. She'd forgotten the simple luxury of human touch, and missed it. Sure, she held Pia all the time, but that wasn't the same as losing herself to the warmth of being held.

"John and I have wondered how you've been." Her hand to his cheek, Helen added, "The anniversary had to have been hard on you, too."

Eyes welling, he nodded. "Sorry I haven't called or anything."

"Everyone deals with these things in their own way."

"Still..." Hands in his pockets, he glanced away.

Helen reloaded the cupcake platter, then slipped her arm around Deacon's waist and led him to the deck, where the party was in full swing.

Loneliness consumed Ellie.

In the past, during everything from Thanksgiving to the Superbowl or Saint Patrick's Day, she'd shared kitchen duties with Tom.

She didn't want to cry on what was supposed to be a happy occasion, but once her tears started, they didn't let up. Snatching about fourteen paper towels, she dashed for the pantry, closing herself inside for the kind of self-indulgent sob fest she usually avoided.

Encompassed in the homey scents of cinnamon and flour, she hugged herself, struggling to recapture the feel of Tom's arms around her.

The door opened. Deacon held a cupcake to his mouth. "There you are! Hey…" Setting the baked good on the nearest shelf, he drew her against his chest, securing her with his powerful arms. She'd wanted so badly to be held, but not by him. Her remembered attraction for him was too strong, filling her with guilt as she all but collapsed against him, soaking in his strength.

"What set this off?"

"B-being alone in the kitchen. You know how Tom loved to cook."

"Yeah." Deacon held her all the tighter. "His manicotti was off the charts."

"Remember his cheesecake?" Ellie sniffed.

"We should make it sometime. You still have all his recipes, right?"

Nodding while blowing her nose, she managed to whisper, "I've thought about making some of his favorite dishes, but it somehow felt wrong."

"Seems to me—" Deacon released her to take a bite of his cupcake "—it'd be like a tribute. Maybe once every month or so, we could have a Taste of Tom night."

Ellie couldn't help but laugh. "Taste of Tom? What an awful name. A tad cannibalistic, don't you think?"

Shrugging, he finished off his cupcake. "Made you laugh. That was really all I wanted."

"Thanks." She meant it. Of all people to pull her out of her funk, Deacon would've been the last person she'd turn to. Surprisingly, she'd been wrong.

For Deacon, watching Pia open her gifts brought on a strange mixture of happiness and sadness. This little girl, more interested in the bows and boxes than the toys, was his child. His flesh and blood. Two months earlier, she'd been a cute kid, but in no way a significant part of his life.

"Adorable, isn't she?" Tom's father paused alongside Deacon. "Looks more like her daddy every day."

Deacon's stomach lurched. "Um, yeah."

"Honestly, I don't know what Helen and I would do without that little girl." He sipped his punch. "Losing Tom was—still is—a special brand of hell, but as long as we have this piece of him, we've got to keep it together, you know?"

Not sure what to say, Deacon scratched his head. "Makes sense."

"Mind helping me?" Ellie held out a trash bag to Deacon. "Who knew fifteen kids under the age of five could generate so much mess?"

"Trust me," John said, "they'll only get worse. When Tom was a teen, we were constantly nagging him to clean his room."

With John off taking pictures of Pia opening more gifts, Deacon said to Ellie, "Thanks for the save. I see what you mean about Tom's folks being attached to Pia."

"Do you blame them?" She stuffed three paper plates in his bag.

"No. Of course, not. But Ell..." He snagged her upper arm. "One of these days, they'll have to know."

She wrenched free. "Not today."

Chapter Five

Heartburn threatening to eat a hole through her stomach, Ellie couldn't believe only an hour earlier she'd actually been comforted by Deacon's presence. Now, with his not so subtle reminder that one day she'd have to tell the Hilliards the truth, she wished more than anything he'd go away.

"Oh my..." Helen studied Pia's next gift—a complex, battery-powered, ride-on pink Hummer. "Deacon, that's awfully extravagant, and not really age appropriate."

"It's perfect," he argued, snatching Pia from her grandmother's lap. "Look, sweetie." He plopped the little girl onto the plastic seat. "You can drive a Humvee just like your daddy's when he's at work."

Ellie cringed.

While all in attendance believed Deacon was referring to the Hummer Tom used to drive, Ellie knew better.

How dare he?

In the pantry, she'd thought they'd reached a truce. Judging by Deacon's current behavior, holding Pia upright in the toy vehicle while making vroom noises, his maturity level wasn't much higher than his daughter's.

"Deacon," Helen said, "I know you mean well, but

the box says this toy has a recommended age of five-year-olds and up."

"Cool!" cried one of the neighbor boys.

Pia had started to cry.

"I'll take her," Ellie said. "She's probably tired."

"I can handle her," Deacon insisted, though Pia wailed louder. "What's the matter, birthday girl? You're not supposed to cry on your big day."

Whether he liked it or not, Ellie took Pia in her arms. "It's okay," she crooned.

"One day, when you're a parent," Helen said to Deacon, "you'll be able to decipher all your child's burps and coos—or in this case, screams."

Ellie, trailed by her mother-in-law, took Pia inside, away from the loud music and other shrieking kids.

Thankfully, Deacon stayed outside.

"That was odd." While Ellie changed Pia's diaper, Helen settled in the nursery's comfy armchair.

"What?" Ellie glanced up from the changing table.

"Deacon's behavior. We haven't heard a peep out of him since Tom's anniversary dinner. Now all of a sudden he shows up, acting like he's Pia's best friend." Inspecting her nails, Helen added, "I don't know about you, but I'm a little offended."

Would this day ever end? "No doubt he feels awkward about leaving your party without saying goodbye."

"Maybe."

By the time Ellie got Pia changed, the baby's eyes were fluttering shut. Poor thing was exhausted. Settling her in her crib, she tiptoed from the room, followed by Helen, who closed the door behind them.

"I used to think highly of Deacon. You know, for all he's overcome." In the kitchen, Helen said, "I'd love a cup of coffee. Should I make an extra-large pot in case anyone else wants some, too?"

"Sure." Ellie sat at one of the counter stools.

"Why do you think Deacon insisted Pia play with such an obviously unsuitable toy?"

Pressing her fingertips to her throbbing forehead, Ellie sighed. "Would you mind if we tabled this topic? I should get back to my guests."

"You go on." The fragrant coffee had started to brew. "I'll be out in a minute."

Back to the melee of running kids and chatting adults, Ellie had just taken a giant stuffed rabbit from chubby Franco, the kindergartner who lived next door, when Deacon paused alongside her. "We need to talk."

"I want the bunny!" Franco hollered.

"Sorry, bud," Deacon told the kid, "but that's Pia's. She got it as a present, remember?"

"It's mine!" Franco insisted.

"There a problem?" A tank-size man Ellie recognized as Franco's dad, Franco Sr., stepped into the argument.

"Yeah," Deacon said. "Your kid stole my kid's rabbit, and he's getting it all sticky."

"Pia's not *your* kid, and how do I know she didn't get frosting on it before my kid even touched it?"

When Deacon's hands fisted, Ellie prayed for peace between the two hulking men.

"You really want to go there, man? If so, I'm more than ready."

Franco Sr. laughed. "You hotshot navy guys are all the same. Acting like you're tough sh—"

"Stop!" Ellie shoved her way between the men.

"Enough's enough. This is a child's party and I'd appreciate both of you leaving."

"I'm not going anywhere," Deacon declared.

"Oh," Franco Sr. retorted, "you're going somewhere, all right, but it's gonna be the ground." He raised his arm to throw a punch, but even Ellie knew that with Deacon's training, he could put the guy in a coma if he wanted.

Deacon grabbed hold of the neighbor's wrist, wrenching his arm far enough backward to make him drop to his knees. "Who's leaving?"

"Franco?" The guy's wife came running to his defense. "Honey, are you all right?"

"Come on." Once again standing, Franco Sr. called to his son. "We're out of here."

"Can I keep this?" Franco Jr. hugged the pink, frosting-coated rabbit.

"Please," Ellie said, "take it and just go."

"Good riddance," Deacon grumbled when the trio left through the back gate.

"What's wrong with you?" she snapped, once the last guest had left—even John and Helen. Ever since the near fight, the other parents had been gathering belongings and children at lightning speed. "This was supposed to have been a happy day. How in the world could you do something so disrespectful to me and Pia as starting a fight over a stupid toy rabbit?"

"For the record—" Deacon stooped to grab a soda can from the lawn "—I stopped the fight. That loser didn't have a chance."

"I swear, I don't even know you."

Grabbing two plastic cups, he said, "That kid stole Pia's present. Who does that? I wasn't going to let him get away with it. Lord knows, she'll have to put up with enough of that kind of crap once she hits her teens."

"Go." Ellie pointed toward the gate.

"Why?" He kept working. "You need help cleaning. Pia's half mine, so I should deal with the aftermath of her party."

Hands on her suddenly throbbing lower back, Ellie said, "You just don't get it, do you? Pia, Helen and John are all I have. I never knew my father, and to this day, my mom is a mean drunk. For me, marrying Tom was life's ultimate do-over." After an almost hysterical laugh mixed with more tears, she added, "Considering the secret I kept from him, I didn't deserve him."

AFTER LEAVING ELLIE, Deacon tried working off his frustration by riding his motorcycle too fast, but traffic never allowed him to get much over sixty.

He next hit his favorite bar, Tipsea's, but while he was nursing straight tequila, his mind's eye focused on Ellie and that sad story about her drunk mother. Suddenly becoming a parent put a lot of pressure on him to get his act together. Most guys had nine months. Sadly, the clock had long run out on Deacon's grace period.

Bob Seger blared from the jukebox.

Cigarette smoke clouded the air.

Garrett and Tristan were on a double date, but Deacon wished they were with him. It had been quite a day, from finding Ellie sobbing in the pantry, to his altercation with her neighbor.

"What's up?" Deacon's favorite bartender, white-haired Maggie, who claimed to be older than the state, rested her forearms on the bar. "You look as worn-out as I feel."

"Thanks." He downed the rest of his drink.

"Refill?"

"Nah." He trailed the tip of his index finger around the rim of his glass. "Trying to cut back. I would like a cheeseburger, though. Extra pickles? And a Coke?"

She winked. "You got it."

After Deacon downed his meal, Maggie stopped by again to refresh his cola. "Planning on telling me what's got you down?"

"Got a few days?"

Laughing, she said, "It's a slow night. How about fifteen minutes?"

The woman had been a maternal figure to him for as long as he'd been at the Virginia Beach base. Knowing she was a friend he could trust, he gave her the highlights of the past months' events, ending with him being Pia's true daddy.

Once he'd finished, Maggie whistled. "I see why you'd need to stay sober—although may not want to."

"What do you think?" Deacon asked. "I get why Ellie is struggling with telling Tom's folks. With their feelings in mind, should I play by Ell's rules and maintain the status quo? Or, while Pia's still young, get to know her like a father should?" Like the father he'd always wished he'd had?

"Hmm…" Drumming her fingers on the wooden bar, Maggie took her sweet time answering. "To my way of thinking, it'd be a shame for that little girl to grow up not having a dad in her life, all because her mom's scared of facing the music."

Leaning in closer, Deacon said, "But in her defense, this goes deeper. It's not just about not wanting to upset

Tom's folks. With him gone, she needs them as much as they need her."

"Don't get me wrong," Maggie said, "they should always be part of Pia and Ellie's lives. But your little girl shouldn't miss out on having a father because of them. Yes, they're going to be upset—very. But even they will eventually agree that Pia needs a father in her life more than they need to hold a grudge."

Deacon wasn't so sure.

"HE DID WHAT?" Ellie switched Pia to her other hip. She hadn't expected to be at the bank for so long.

"Mr. Murphy set up an account for your daughter. He's already deposited several thousand dollars. Pia is the primary account holder, but you will also need to sign all documentation, since she's a minor. Mr. Murphy is also on the account."

"But I don't want his money," Ellie argued, staring at the assistant manager, who'd phoned that morning, requesting she stop by her local First Federal branch.

"Please," the woman said, pushing stylish black glasses higher on her pert nose. "If you'll have a seat, we'll sort this out."

While Ms. Davenport typed on her computer, Ellie wished the canned samba music playing over the intercom would stop. She wished the flowery potpourri in a bowl on Ms. Davenport's desk wasn't so strong. Most of all, she wished she'd never given in to her conscience's demand to tell Deacon about Pia.

From his territorial stance at her party, and now this, Tom's parents would know the truth far sooner than Ellie wanted.

"Ma'am," the clerk said, "from what I can see, you

have full access to the money, to use however you see fit for Pia's benefit. We deal with divorce cases all the time and—"

"No. I was never married to this man. What gave you that idea?"

Her cheeks reddened. "Sorry. I assumed, since Mr. Murphy listed himself as Pia's father, that you two were... Well, again, I'm very sorry."

Feeling queasy and entirely too hot, Ellie used the passbook she'd been given as a fan. Pia grabbed it, promptly deciding to chew the corner.

"No, sweetie." Taking it from her, Ellie tucked it into the purse she'd slung over her shoulder. To Ms. Davenport, she said, "Thank you for your help."

"This is a good thing," the woman said with an exaggerated smile. "Who doesn't love free money?"

Me. Especially when, knowing Deacon, there were no doubt major strings attached.

EARLY THAT EVENING, having left Pia with her grandparents, Ellie broke the speed limit getting to Deacon's apartment.

Once there, she pounded on the door.

"Hey," Garrett said. "Long time no—"

Ellie brushed past him. "Where's Deacon?"

"Whoa." Garrett flattened himself against the open door. "Nice to see you, too."

"Deacon!" The three-bedroom apartment wasn't that big. Where could he be?

"Um..." Garrett cleared his throat. "If you'd made time for the most basic of pleasantries, I could've told you Deacon's not here."

"Oh." After an awkward apology, she asked, "Mind telling me where he is?"

"Northport Beach. He parks his bike behind that abandoned ice cream shop."

AFTER TEN HOURS in a dry suit for more training, the last spot Deacon would've expected himself to go after the endless day was the beach. But lately, it was the only place he felt calm. He ran until his legs ached. Until his calves screamed.

Finally back where he'd started, he collapsed on the sand, staring up at the rising moon.

"Deacon!" Just the tone of Ellie's voice made him wince. What the hell was she doing at his private sanctuary, and what had he done wrong now?

She stood next to him, hands on her hips, her petite frame lost in a hoodie Deacon recognized as Tom's. Wind whipped her dark hair about her face, reminding him how he'd once slipped his fingers through those tousled waves.

"Why did you set up a bank account for Pia? Tom had plenty of life insurance, and I don't need your money. What if someone at the bank talks? You know how this town loves to gossip. Can you imagine the nightmare my life's going to be when all my friends discover I slept with my dead husband's best friend?"

"You didn't used to be this selfish." On his feet, Deacon strolled toward the surf, intent on washing sand from his feet.

"Selfish?" Chasing after him, she hollered, "What do you think you're being? Doing everything in your power to turn my life upside down?"

"Have you ever looked at this situation from my point

of view?" He slicked water from his shins. "My dad treated me like a dog compared to my wonder brother, who could do no wrong. Peter was everything I wasn't. Football star, Eagle Scout, the son with a stellar future. The more he achieved, the more I screwed up. Arrested for possession, underage drinking, busting into our school. I was every parent's worst nightmare and my folks weren't afraid to let me know it. Fast-forward a dozen years and I'm doing all right for myself. Gotta admit I never saw myself having a kid, but now that I do, I want Pia to know, deep inside—" he patted his chest "—that she's unconditionally loved. She doesn't have to do a thing other than exist to earn her father's love."

Eyes tearing in the light of the rising moon, long hair flowing behind her, Ellie looked beautiful and vulnerable at the same time. "I want that, too. That's why I told you the truth. But now that our secret's out, I'm scared of the consequences," she said. Her voice had been barely loud enough for him to hear.

"Me, too." He went to her, planning to enfold her in a hug, but at the last moment, he couldn't. His attraction for her was still too primal. His respect for her husband—his best friend—too strong. "I like Tom's folks. I'm willing to give you time to make an official announcement, but I'm also planning to try being the kind of dad I wanted my own father to be." Hands in his pockets, Deacon locked his gaze with hers. "Money in the bank means nothing. Anyone can provide financial support. I don't have a clue if I can be a decent dad. All I know is that I won't be able to live with myself if I don't at least try."

Ellie's heart went out to him. Tom had told her a little

about Deacon's upbringing, but she really knew nothing about his past, the early years that had formed the man he was today. "Interesting," she mused, "that we both had lousy parents, only on opposite ends of the spectrum. I remember feeling hopeless, but I fought that demon by overachieving. You might've initially chosen defiance, Deacon, but look at you now. You've devoted your life to serving your country and saving people who can't save themselves. You're reliable and hardworking, and I can only imagine how proud your parents and brother must be of you now."

"Yeah…" He rubbed his stubbled jaw. "Might've gone that way, only there's one problem. Peter's dead."

"Oh, Deacon…" She couldn't help but squeeze him in a hug. "I'm sorry. What happened?"

Almost as if he couldn't stand being touched, he pulled free. "Car accident."

Her throat knotted from not only his story, but the notion that she'd alienated him to the point that he didn't want her comfort, Ellie asked, "Your parents must've turned to you after that, right?"

He laughed. "Far from it. Not only was I behind the wheel the night Peter died, but I had the misfortune to live."

Chapter Six

Deacon rode his bike as if the devil were dragging him home.

Why had he told Ellie about Peter? He'd never told a soul, not even Tom. The day of his brother's funeral, Deacon had been in intensive care. The day he'd been released from the hospital, he'd enlisted. Left town without a word to anyone.

Since then, he received cards and calls from his mother on his birthday and Christmas, but he had yet to hear from his dad. The bastard. Clint Murphy wanted to blame him for Peter's death. Well, Deacon knew it to be a horrible accident. It'd been raining and a semi had lost control, ramming the car's passenger side. Deacon had been driving under the speed limit, actually enjoying his brother's company. Peter had been home from his second year at UCLA. A star kicker, he'd led the football team to a national championship, and pro scouts were already knocking on his door.

Their father had attended every one of Peter's games, no matter how far he'd had to travel. Their house had been filled with memorabilia. Newspapers and programs. Photos and pennant flags and stuffed Bruins bears.

Deacon's dad had played for Colorado State, but never had the success of his oldest son. To say he lived vicariously through him would be the understatement of the century. To say that, when Peter died, he also gave up on life wouldn't be in the least bit melodramatic.

While Deacon felt sorry for his mother, living the rest of her life with just a shell of her husband, she'd never so much as lifted a finger to convince the man he was wrong to blame his younger son. And for that, Deacon didn't care if he ever saw either of them again.

On and on he drove, at a dangerous speed. He was well into North Carolina when he finally pulled over at a rest stop and took a nap beneath a tree.

A few hours later, back on his bike, nourished from a protein bar he'd found stashed in his jacket pocket, he headed for home, making it to the base just in time for morning roll call.

Throughout the day, he performed his training duties to the level of perfection expected of a seasoned SEAL. After that, he rode to Ellie's.

He not only needed to hold his daughter, to reassure himself he wasn't anything like his father, but he had the oddest craving to see Pia's mom. To hear her sweet voice tell him everything would be okay.

Trouble was, from her point of view, things couldn't be further from okay. Yet again Deacon found himself in the position of being resented for living, when the man Ellie wanted was dead.

"HEY." Ellie opened her back door to find Deacon standing there. Though her pulse was racing, she wasn't sure how to feel about his appearance. Their last meeting had covered a lot of emotional ground—too much. Part of her still felt raw from his revelations.

Motorcycle helmet in his hands, he said, "Hope it's okay, me stopping by. I mean, I know I should've called, but—"

"As long as you behave, you're always welcome."

He winced. "Guess that means you won't be offering tequila for dinner?"

"No, but I did make tortilla soup." Flashing a half smile she hoped masked her nerves, she added, "It kinda goes with your Mexican theme."

"If you're sharing, I'll sure eat. Sounds good." When he entered, his bare forearm brushed hers, launching a whole new set of problems. The night of Pia's conception, the chemistry Ellie felt for Deacon had taken on a life of its own. His slightest touch had sparked shimmering heat and awareness of his size and strength and masculinity. He was the kind of man who'd made her feel all-woman. Not that Tom hadn't been a wonderful lover. But where her husband had made her feel safe, Deacon had made her feel wicked, in a wholly pleasurable way.

Pia kicked in her high chair, squealing and holding out her arms. "Up! Up!"

Ellie started to go to her, but Deacon cut her off. "Let me." Raising Pia high in the air launched a fit of adorable baby giggles. "Vroom, you're an airplane."

While Deacon played with their daughter, Ellie set the table with more care than she would for just herself and Pia. She used colorful place mats and set out the good glassware. Deacon's opening up had been a turning point for her. She now felt an odd kinship with him, due to their equally lousy upbringings. She'd escaped hers, but sensed he stilled lived with the demons of his.

"You two ready to eat?" she asked, after placing a bowl of freshly grated cheddar on the table to sprinkle on the soup.

"Smells amazing." After returning Pia to her high chair, Deacon asked, "Anything you need me to do?"

"Want to try your hand at feeding a two-year-old soup?"

Though a brief look of fear passed over his face, he gamely took the plastic bowl Ellie offered, as well as the child-size spoon. "I just hold it up to her mouth?"

Nodding, Ellie said, "She's great at feeding herself, so as much as you can, just sort of guide her. That way, she'll hopefully end up with at least half in her tummy rather than decorating her clothes."

"Gotcha." With a focused expression, he turned to the task, as serious as if preparing for a top secret mission. Brows knitted, biting his lower lip, he guided Pia's spoon with pinpoint precision.

Ellie couldn't help but laugh.

"What?" He glanced in her direction. "I haven't spilled a drop."

"That's why it's funny. It's okay to have fun."

"Now I'm confused." He leaned back in his chair. "You told me not to get it on her."

Pia started to fuss.

"Like this." Ellie covered his hand with hers, guiding it toward the girl's open mouth. A little of the broth dribbled on the high chair's plastic tray, but in the time Deacon had taken to manage one perfect spoonful, Ellie worked in three.

What she hadn't counted on was another rush of

awareness stemming from touching him. Cheeks flushed, she retreated to her own side of the table, noting, "Too much spice in the soup."

Spooning a bite from his bowl, Deacon said, "Tastes just right to me."

Once Pia had eaten her fill, and started happily feeding herself oyster crackers, Ellie said, "Our talk last night has been on my mind all day."

Meeting her gaze, he said, "Me, too. I said too much. Dumping on you."

"Not at all." She ached for what he'd been through. "I'm honored you trusted me enough to share."

"IF YOU FOLD THAT FAST every day I'm going to have to give you a raise." Ada, dressed in white wool Chanel, sat at the register, flipping through *Vogue*. "What—or should I ask, who—has you so driven?"

"Well…" It was on the tip of Ellie's tongue to tell her friend morning vitamins had her so peppy, but she wasn't in the mood for games. "Deacon came over last night."

"Nice." Ada tossed her magazine on the glass checkout counter. "Or is this an anger-fueled energy burst?"

"That's just it." Ellie folded colorful designer T-shirts even faster. "We actually had a fun time. I made soup, and for at least a few bites he fed Pia."

"Why only a few bites?"

"He was too slow, struggling to do a perfect job. But in retrospect, my even saying that makes me out to be a serious bitch. I was the one wanting Pia to have her dad in her life, but now that she does, I'm constantly berating him even though he's trying so hard. Even worse, whenever he so much as accidentally brushes against me, I feel all tingly from my belly to my toes. What do I do with that? Deacon was Tom's best friend. There can't *ever* be romance between us again."

Ada took a few seconds to mull that over. "Why?"

"Seriously?" Ellie abandoned her task in favor of collapsing in the nearest armchair. "The guilt of even finding him attractive is eating me alive."

"Let's break this down." Leaving the register, Ada took the seat beside Ellie. "Kinda hard to deny the guy is beyond sexy. Another fact you're ignoring is that even though Tom died, you're very much alive. Do you actually believe he'd wish you to be alone forever, mourning the loss of what you two shared?"

ONE WEEK INTO OCTOBER, Deacon showed up at the library where Ellie attended her weekly widow support group. They'd worked out a routine where he took Pia for ice cream, or strolling in the mall for an hour, and then they met up again. An hour was barely enough time to get the child into her car seat. No way did it allow for real bonding. But at this point in his short-lived parenting career, did he even know what that meant?

"Sorry we're late." Ellie ran up to where he sat on his bike. The wind carried a hint of her flowery perfume and an icy nip. Pia was bundled up to her nose. "This one's been cranky. I'm afraid she's coming down with a cold."

"Have you taken her to a doctor?"

"Not yet."

Ellie passed Pia to him. The little girl's weight felt so good in his arms, and being around Ellie irrationally made his spirit soar. Lord, how he looked forward to Thursdays.

"So far, she's just had sniffles and a slight cough. No fever."

"Still…"

"She's fine." After handing him her car keys—Deacon couldn't exactly transport a toddler on his bike—she said, "Last week, a friend in my group, Mary, asked me to grab a coffee with her after our session. Would you be okay watching Pia for two hours?"

"Sure." Nothing would make him happier.

Ellie hugged her daughter, then hurried into the warmth of the Victorian-style library.

He was fastening Pia's safety harness when it occurred to Deacon that the transition would've been smoother if he'd just met Ellie at her car. The lot was full, so she hadn't been able to park beside him.

"See, peanut?" he said to his little girl. "I've got to get a handle on more of these kinds of details. That way, you wouldn't have had to come out into the cold."

When he left her to get behind the wheel, she cried.

"There's no crying on Pia and Daddy's fun night." Reaching into the backseat, he jiggled her boot-covered foot.

Apparently not caring, she cried all the harder.

Swell.

Having extra time, Deacon headed for a place he'd carefully spent his whole life avoiding—Wacky Willie's Pizza. He'd seen ads and the place looked mortifying. But for kids, he supposed it was playtime Mecca.

Even the parking was insane, and Deacon finally found a spot that felt like a mile from the front door. Though he carefully bundled Pia to protect her from the wind, she was still crying.

"Hey," he said, bouncing her in his arms, "do you have any idea where we're going? Kid heaven."

"Mommeee!" She cried so hard snot ran from her nose, and Deacon had forgotten the diaper bag that Ellie had told him to never be without.

"Hold on, peanut…" He jogged with her back to the car, found tissue in the bag, cleaned up Pia's nose, then started their mission anew.

While he stood in line for pizza, Pia was still weepy.

He removed her coat, mittens, scarf and hat, shoving them all in the magic bag. Who knew kids carried as much gear as any SEAL? "That better?"

She shook her head, then dropped her head on his shoulder. Melted didn't begin to describe what Pia resting on him did to his heart. "Mommy…"

"I know, sweetie. We'll see her soon. Right now, you're going to play with *Daddy,* okay?" Whenever he was with her, he worked in his official title, in the hopes of her one day using it. It sounded good. He just selfishly wished she'd occasionally pine for him the way she did Ellie. "Daddy's fun."

By the time Deacon bought a large Extreminater pizza, sodas and a sackful of game tokens, he was already worn-out. Between blasting pop music, screeching kids of all ages and a scent vaguely reminiscent of burned cheese, frosting and dirty diapers, he'd learned Wacky Willie's should be the go-to punishment for terrorists.

He found an empty spot, set down the food tray, then put Pia in the chair beside his. Only her head barely reached the top of the table. And she was still sniffling.

Not seeing any high chairs, he just went with the

awkward setup. "Look." He waved a small slice of pizza in front of her. "You love this stuff, don't you?"

She grabbed it from him, instantly fisting it into a gooey mess.

"Deacon?"

"Oh, hello, sir." He looked up to see Commander Duncan and his wife with two of their freckled grandkids in tow. From base picnics, Deacon knew them to be school-aged.

"Reginald, Franklin," the commander said, "this is one of my finest men, Chief Petty Officer Deacon Murphy. He's a SEAL."

"Whoa! Can I have your autograph?" the taller of the two asked.

"Um, SEALs really don't do that," Deacon said, trying to keep Pia upright and contain her wadded pizza. "But I'll bet your grandfather would let you come on base and play with some of our toys. We've got really good ones."

"That'd be awesome!" The boys gave each other high fives.

"Deacon? Isn't that little Pia Hilliard?" Paula asked.

"Yes, ma'am. I watch her for Ellie on Thursday nights."

Her expression almost hopeful, the flawlessly dressed woman gazed at him. "Are you two an *item?*"

"No," he replied with an exaggerated shake of his head. "I'm just helping a friend."

"That's awfully sweet of you." Nodding to Pia, she said, "You do know they have booster seats for children Pia's age? Makes it much easier for you to manage a wriggling toddler. And for future reference, most children prefer plain cheese pizza."

"Now, Mother." The commander came to Deacon's

aid. "My boy here is capable of taking out an entire camp of terrorists on his own. He shouldn't also be expected to know the finer points of parenting, especially for a child who doesn't even belong to him."

"HAVE FUN?" Ellie asked when Deacon pulled the car up in front of the library.

"Not sure I'd go that far," he admitted, unfastening his seat belt. "And I apologize for Pia being such a mess. I did the best I could, cleaning her with wipes, but the pizza in her hair won't come out."

"Hmm…" Ellie walked around to Pia's side of the car, opening the door to inspect her child. Face and hair greasy, reeking of peppers and onions… She had never seen her daughter in such a state. "Where did you two go?"

"Wacky Willie's, aka hell."

"Mommeee!"

Ellie reached for Pia. "I know, pumpkin. You're tired, huh?" To Deacon, she asked, "Where are her mittens? It's below freezing."

"Probably in the diaper bag."

"Which is where?" Ellie always kept it on the floor in front of Pia's seat.

Deacon slapped his forehead. "I grabbed her coat and scarf out of it, but must've left the bag under our table. I was kind of distracted."

"By what?" Closing the rear door, Ellie met Deacon on the driver's side.

"The base commander and his wife showed up with their grandkids. Paula straight-out asked if we're dating."

Groaning, Ellie covered her face with her free hand.

"I'm not ready for this. You know how gossipy this town is. See? This is exactly the kind of thing I've been hoping to avoid."

"That's all well and good, but the truth would've shut her up."

Nausea nearly doubled Ellie over. Of course, Deacon was right. Full disclosure would've allowed him to admit he was Pia's father. But that also would've led to a whole new set of issues—explaining that Pia's conception had occurred before Ellie had even met Tom. But did anyone aside from Helen and John honestly need that much information?

His hand on her back, Deacon asked, "You all right?"

"Yeah." She straightened. "Maybe." She laughed. "Honestly, I don't know."

"I know the feeling, but somehow, everything's going to be okay. We haven't done anything wrong. And the more I'm with Pia, the more everything feels right."

"I'm glad," Ellie managed to answer with a shaky sigh. And she was. Having lost Tom, Pia deserved every shred of happiness she could get. And Deacon deserved to get to know his daughter after missing out on so much of her life because of Ellie's cowardice. As for herself, Ellie more often than not felt nothing but disgust for the way she'd continually botched the whole situation.

"Sorry I forgot the diaper bag. I'll run to Willie's to get Pia's stuff, then drop it by the house."

"That'd be great. Thanks." Even better would be if he stuck around to share Pia's bathtime.

AFTER DEACON LEFT Pia's diaper bag—declining Ellie's invitation to stay, on the grounds that he and Garrett had plans—she knelt in front of the tub while scrubbing assorted pizza toppings from their daughter's hair.

Plans? Why was she suddenly consumed by thoughts of what those might entail? Drinking? Dancing? Body shots with hot young things? Where Deacon was concerned, Ellie's imagination grew fertile, as did jealousy she had no right to feel.

"Hope you at least had fun while getting this dirty."

Pia patted the bubbles and squealed.

"Wish you were old enough to tell me what you and your dad talk about." Ellie began rinsing no-tear shampoo from Pia's hair. "When I was your age, I suppose I saw my father. I don't remember. Mom didn't start drinking heavily until I was in third grade." She used a plastic cup to rinse, smoothing Pia's hair as she worked. "I remember because we had a huge Christmas program and your mommy was the star—literally." Ellie laughed. "My class made a big holiday tree and I got to stand at the very top. There was one song about a cold winter wind and I had to sway." Her throat tightened. "I was on top of a ladder, behind risers. Some kids wore green to be branches, and some wore red to be ornaments. I was the only one wearing yellow. Our teacher held the ladder while I swayed—you know, to make sure I didn't fall. But out in the audience, my mom couldn't see that. I guess—" she wagged Pia's pink duck "—I should be flattered she cared, but right in the middle of the song, my mom jumped out of her seat, stumbled past all the other kids' parents, climbed up onto the stage and then up the risers. At the top, she grabbed me, tossing me over her shoulder and yelling at my teacher about how she shouldn't have put me in danger."

Ellie had been old enough to realize everyone in that

gymnasium was staring. The next morning, she had gone to a meeting with the counselor and her mom. Her mother had been sober and apologetic, explaining how confused she'd been on prescription cough syrup.

She had been a master at disguising her alcohol usage.

Ellie lost count of how many times school officials had asked if her mom was drinking, but Ellie always covered for her, knowing the alternative was foster care.

"Sorry to be a Debbie Downer during what's usually a fun time for us." At least Ellie's mind was temporarily off Deacon.

Pia had ignored Ellie's speech, intent on scooping bubbles into measuring cups.

"With Halloween coming, we'll be having lots of fun. You like fun, don't you?"

Pia grinned. "Daddy fun! Daddy fun!"

As much as Ellie hated to admit it, she had to agree. Which was a problem, considering how she was all over the map emotionally. Scared of Helen and John never speaking to her again once they learned Pia wasn't theirs. Guilt-ridden over wishing she'd never told Deacon the truth. Ashamed by the fact that every time he was near, her body hummed with attraction.

Chapter Seven

Halloween night, while Tom's parents and dozens of friends and neighbors played with Pia, Ellie helped herself to more vampire punch. Though she'd been worried about John and Helen thinking it odd that Deacon wanted to join them, they'd been gracious, adopting a more-the-merrier attitude.

"Help me with a refill?" Deacon held out his black plastic goblet.

"Sure," Ellie said over blaring, kid-friendly monster tunes, the whole while praying he didn't notice the silver ladle trembling in her hand. "Having fun?"

"Oddly enough, yeah." His gorgeous smile made her stomach flip.

With her dressed as Red Riding Hood and him as a fireman, they stood side by side at the deck railing, staring out at the dark ocean view.

The night was clear, and with Pia off playing with friends, the stars and moon provided a far more romantic backdrop than Ellie would've liked. Her whole side nearest Deacon tingled, and she vascillated between enjoying the sensation and wishing it would stop.

Deacon sipped his punch. "This place is awesome."

"Agreed." Tom's dad had made a considerable fortune in stocks and was now retired. When Tom was stationed in Virginia Beach, his parents had moved, too. Though the modern home was mostly made of glass, Helen had enough antiques mixed into her eclectic decor that her high-end Halloween decorations managed to look both elegant and festive. "Pia's loving this."

"I'm getting a kick out of seeing her interact with other kids. Did you see her face when Austin tried scaring her?"

"Yes." Ellie laughed. "But she wasn't having it. I caught myself holding my breath, waiting for her to cry, but she didn't back down."

"Yep." Deacon puffed out his chest. "That's the SEAL in her."

"Stop!" Ellie gave him a playful pummel, then abruptly stopped. What was she doing? To anyone viewing them, they must look like a couple flirting!

"You know it's true." When he continued their fun by nudging her side, she scooted away a good six inches.

"Maybe so, but I thank my stars every day that I had a girl, and not a boy who wants to follow in his father's footsteps."

"Aw, don't say that." Deacon's tone had sobered. "Sure, being a SEAL is dangerous, but a lot more than sweat went into earning my Trident. I learned about honor and trust and never giving up. Pia's going to learn all of that up front—from you and me."

"I—I hope so." Damn her racing pulse. What was it about Deacon vowing to share in teaching good values that made Ellie's knees weak and stomach flutter? Then he had to go and meet her gaze, holding it as if to seal an unspoken promise to always do right by their girl.

Hastily dropping her gaze, Ellie reminded herself how much she loved John and Helen—far more than she ever had her own parents. Once the Hilliards learned that their son had had nothing to do with Pia's DNA, would they drop Ellie and her daughter cold? The thought terrified Ellie—so much that to stop her punch from spilling she held her quaking goblet with both hands.

"You all right?"

She should've known nothing escaped Deacon. After setting his own drink on the railing, he curved his hands over hers. His touch was warm and solid and entirely too reassuring—a horrible development, considering her need to stay away. "You're shaking."

"Cold," she said.

"Try this…." He removed his jacket, settling it over her shoulders. It still held his heat and the faint citrus-and-leather scent of his aftershave. "Better?"

"Yes. Thanks." Deeply inhaling, Ellie told herself it was only the festive occasion stirring up riotous feelings of attraction.

"I hate even asking this, but—"

Good Lord, was he wanting to kiss her?

"—does Pia seem to enjoy my company as much as I do hers?"

Ellie gave herself a mental slap. *What's wrong with you?* Why would she for even one second assume Deacon wanted to kiss her? Struggling to regain her composure, she confessed, "The night you took her for pizza, during her bath she told me—and I quote, 'Daddy fun!'"

"Seriously?" His expression brightened. "You're not making that up?"

Ellie shook her head. "She's crazy about you. Her whole personality is changing for the better."

"Thank you for sharing that…" He took her drink and set it on the rail, then grasped her hands again and squeezed. "As much as I need Pia, you have no idea how much it means that she also needs me. Yes, I'm going to make mistakes with her, but if you'll let me see even more of her, I really think it'd be a good thing."

"Me, too." She released him, not because touching Deacon was unpleasant, but rather because doing so produced the oddest cravings to draw him in for a proper hug. "When it fits your schedule, feel free to stop by in the afternoons. Saturdays are usually good, too."

When he flashed his most irresistible, white-toothed smile, then stepped toward her for that hug she'd been craving, Ellie's body quivered in anticipation. Until he abruptly drew back.

"Helen—" he took a sausage roll from the platter she held out "—thanks again for having me. This has been way more fun than the bar everyone else went to."

Tom's mother got Ellie's hug. "You're, ah, welcome."

Once Helen left, Deacon asked, "She seem cool to you?"

"I suppose. Why?"

He shook his head. "Just a vibe."

For Ellie, the rest of the night took on a bittersweet tone. Most everyone present save her and Deacon were paired up. Hugs and kisses and canoodling abounded. Ellie keenly missed her husband, and no amount of punch would mask that fact.

Worse, watching Pia interact with Deacon only further warmed Ellie's heart.

"Boo!" he teased, helping her pretend to fly like a ghost. "You're so scary!"

Each time he swung their daughter through the air, Pia squealed and giggled. "Daddy fun! Daddy fun!"

Ellie cringed, hearing her shout the words, but she needn't have worried.

Helen slipped an arm around her and sighed. "I've read about this in grief books. Poor little Pia is substituting Deacon for Tom."

THAT NIGHT it took Ellie a long time to fall asleep. When ten-thirty came and went with her eyes still refusing to shut, she wandered into the nursery to check on Pia, who slept soundly beneath the pink quilt Nana Helen had made her.

In the living room, Ellie lit the gas log fire and the lamp beside the sofa. Then she did something she knew she shouldn't, taking her favorite photo scrapbooks from the entertainment-center shelves. Curled beneath an afghan on the sofa, she flipped through pages documenting happier times. Wedding photos. Her first Christmas with Tom and his family, the Hilliards' house decorated with so many evergreen boughs and peppermint candles even the air had smelled festive. Moving into the house with boxes everywhere, and Deacon had taken a candid shot of her and Tom in an embrace. They'd been bone-deep tired, but happy. So very happy. Then came Pia, seven pounds, six ounces of sheer beauty. Up until then, Ellie had only *thought* she'd been happy. With her little family, she'd never felt more complete. Pia's first birthday had been spent at Helen and John's, on the beach. A cookout, complete with a Jupiter Jump for the bigger kids. Would Ellie ever again experience such a perfect day?

A knock on the door jolted her from her memories.

Heart racing, she peered around the front door curtains, relieved to see Deacon, yet concerned. No good news ever came this late at night.

"What's wrong?" she asked, ushering him in from the cold.

"Nothing. Everything." He shrugged. "Couldn't sleep, so I was out riding around, noticed your lights on and thought I'd check if you were all right."

"Of course. Fine. But you're shivering. Come sit by the hearth and I'll make you some cocoa."

"Sounds good."

"What's the matter with you?" she scolded, removing his cold leather jacket to replace it with the afghan she'd just used. Once he was adequately wrapped, she headed for the kitchen. "It's too chilly to be riding your bike."

"You're right, but it's the only ride I have. In the summer, she's a sexy beast, but this time of year…" He shook his head.

Turning on the fire beneath her kettle, she mused, "You could grow up and get a nice, safe SUV. What it lacks in sex appeal and speed it'll make up for in heated seats and a great stereo."

He laughed. "Gotta admit a heated seat would be heaven about now."

"You know—" she opened packets of gourmet cocoa, dumping the contents into mugs "—I'm not sure why I didn't think of this sooner, but why don't you drive Tom's Jeep?"

"No way," he said with a firm shake of his head. "Wouldn't seem right."

"Why not? It's just sitting in the garage. I keep meaning to put an ad in the paper, but can't quite bring myself to do it."

Holding the blanket around his shoulders, he joined her in the kitchen. "What if I bought it? That way, I could have a safety seat already installed for the munchkin. Would make for easier transfer times."

"Sounds good," she said over the kettle's whistle. "Make me an offer."

By the time they'd added mini marshmallows to their drinks, they'd worked out a mutually beneficial deal, with Ellie agreeing to house Deacon's bike in the garage.

Seated on the opposite end of the sofa from him, steaming mug in hand, Ellie said, "When Pia called you daddy in front of Helen at the party, I thought for sure she'd guess our secret. You don't know how sad it makes me that it never even occurred to her that you *could* be Pia's dad. This only shows how much more devastated she'll be when the time comes to let her and John know."

"You need to give Tom's folks more credit. They might be stronger than you think." He shrugged off the blanket.

"Maybe…" Ellie folded the blanket into a neat square, setting it on the sofa back. "Maybe I'm the one needing more time."

"Which I'm giving." His tone changed, softened. "I've turned my life upside down for you girls—not that I'm complaining, but I can't wait to shout from the rooftops Pia is mine."

"I told you you're welcome to spend as much time with her as you'd like." Ellie hadn't meant her tone to be short, but this wasn't an issue on which she could be pressured. "By Christmas, who knows? Maybe everything will be different. But please, for now, let's take things slow. Ease Pia—and Helen and John—into our new routine."

"Christmas. We'll tell them then. Shake on it?" He held out his hand like a challenge. Did she dare accept?

Pressing her palm against his, she felt a jolt of awareness. Achy tension lodged in her throat. Heat pooled in her limbs. Why wouldn't her attraction for him end? Why did she hold him longer than she rightfully should?

"You're folding fast again." Though the store was loaded with customers whose designer purses proclaimed they had money to spend, Ada stopped on her way to the register to harass her employee. "Have another fun night with Deacon?"

"Long story." Ellie stopped tidying sweaters to help a customer waving from the dressing room find more sizes. "Ring up Mrs. Viera and I'll tell you all about it."

Thirty minutes later, the shop was empty—a luxury with Christmas fast approaching. Warm sun streamed through the plate glass windows and Coldplay provided a mellow vibe through hidden speakers.

"Okay, girl." Ada sat at the counter, sorting mail. "Let's hear it. What'd that fine man of yours do this time?"

"He's not mine," Ellie protested, placing a returned dress back on the rack. "Far from it. Can you believe he wants a deadline for telling John and Helen? Christmas. Is he soulless? We can't deliver that kind of news over the holidays. I don't know why I didn't think of that when he brought it up."

"Hmm…" Chewing the cap of her ballpoint, Ada murmured, "No doubt you were distracted by his eyes.

Any chance of holding him off until the January doldrums?"

"I can try. I was stupid to agree, but I really was caught in his stare and I—"

"Back up the truck." Ada abandoned her latest invoice. "You were *caught in his stare?* What does that mean?"

"You know…" Heat crept up Ellie's cheeks. "He was gazing at me so intensely and I couldn't look away. It was awful."

"Oh. Being stared down by a *GQ*-handsome man. Truly horrifying." Ellie's supposed friend burst out laughing.

"I shouldn't have even told you." Returning to the sweaters, Ellie said, "I know this all must seem crazy to you, but I was once *with* this guy, you know? I remember all too well what he's capable of, and have no wish to revisit that place."

"If that's true, then how come your only thoughts these days seem centered around him? Have you even called that alcoholic outreach program I signed you up to help at? They could really use you over the holidays."

"Yes, *Mom*. I've been working with the nicest woman, Pandora, for over a month. She's making great strides toward getting her life in order."

"Good." After depositing the mail on her office desk, Ada joined Ellie at the sweater table. "I know this whole Deacon thing may be moving too fast for your liking, but stop being afraid of what you feel for him, Ell. He seems like a sweetheart, and Pia clearly adores him."

"He is a sweetheart, but Deacon was also Tom's best

friend. I can't stop thinking that by even appreciating Deacon's smile, I'm cheating on my husband."

"Girl..." Ada shook her head. "You've got issues."

WHEN DEACON PULLED INTO the only empty space in front of the dress shop where Ellie worked, he saw through the windows that though it was past closing time, there were at least five customers still wandering among the racks. Ellie stood at the register, smiling and chatting and in general shredding his insides. "Mommy looks pretty, doesn't she, Pia?"

She clapped in her car seat. "Mommy play!"

"No, sweetie, she's doing her job, but we can play."

"Daddy fun fun!"

Deacon chuckled. "That's what all the girls say."

He turned off the Jeep, then climbed out from behind the wheel to grab Pia from her safety seat.

It'd been a gorgeous day, and though it was already dark at a little past six, the air remained balmy. "What do you want to do?"

"Play!"

In hopes of playing catch, Deacon grabbed the pink Nerf football he'd bought her a few days earlier. Pia pointed at the store. "Mommy!"

"Yep, there she is, but sweetie, Mommy's super busy."

"Mommy play with Pia!" She kicked and added a whiny edge to her tone. Never a good thing. Deacon could now comfortably tackle any diaper emergency, but tantrums were still a bit out of his league.

"Okay. First, great big-girl sentence. Second, Mommy's helping those ladies buy dresses." He pointed into the shop. "See?"

Far from his pep talk motivating his daughter to play football, she tossed her head back for a full-on wail.

"Swell…" When a jiggle-hug combo failed to calm her, Deacon knew he was in over his head. "How about we go inside Mommy's store, but just watch her help the ladies?"

"Yes." Already at the entrance, Pia thankfully reduced her volume to huffing whimpers.

"Hey, you two." Ellie's expression brightened when they approached the counter. Deacon knew better than to believe her smile was meant for him, but that didn't stop him from hoping.

"Aw, she's adorable," a leggy blonde said from her spot in the four-deep checkout line.

"Thanks," Deacon and Ellie said at the same time.

Ellie's smile? Gone.

"How old is she?" a stacked brunette asked, squeezing Pia's sneakered foot.

"A little past two," Deacon said.

"Mommy play!" The ladies all laughed when Pia held out her arms toward her mom.

"We'll play in a little bit, pumpkin. First I need to help these nice people buy dresses."

"Oh." She pouted, only to turn a faint, teary-eyed smile toward Deacon. "Daddy play?"

He gave her a hug and pressed a kiss to her forehead. "I'd love to."

Setting Pia on her feet, he guided her toward the store's seating area. Finally, he'd get to play catch.

Minutes later, with Deacon sitting on the floor and Pia chasing the ball when she missed, a good time was had by all without Mommy being interrupted.

In between throws, Deacon stole looks at Ellie, admiring her polished navy suit and the way she'd twisted her hair into a fancy pile on her head. This business side of her was seriously hot. Knowing it was not an issue he should be dwelling on, he focused on their daughter until the last customer was finally helped and Ada had locked the door.

"Whew." Ellie's best friend fanned her hand in front of her face. "That was intense, but fun." She winked at Ellie. "Christmas bonus time is going to be great. Thanks for all your help."

"Thank you for that bonus." Ellie returned the wink before scooping her daughter into her arms. "I missed you."

"No, Mommy! Me play Daddy!" Pia bucked and wriggled, until Ellie eventually set her down. The toddler chased after her ball, then pitched it to Deacon.

"Nice one," he said, before tossing it back. To Ellie he said, "If you'd told me you were going to need more time, you should've called. I could've kept her out of your hair."

"Thanks, but this doesn't happen all that often." Expression pinched, she looked from their daughter to him, then back to Pia, who was again on the chase.

"Just saying, the offer stands if you need me."

"I appreciate it." The ball had vanished beneath a rack of long, sequined gowns. Their daughter dropped to her belly to squirm after it. "Pia, hon, let's go."

"No!"

Ada emerged from her office, purse in one hand, cell phone in the other. "I don't know about you two, but I could use a martini. Ready?"

"We soon will be." On his feet, Deacon went fishing for Pia beneath the dress rack.

"No! My ball! My ball!" the toddler kicked and wailed.

"You stay with Mommy and I'll get it," Deacon assured her.

Ada checked her nails. "This is why I opt out of children or pets. They're cute, but only from a distance."

Deacon soon had the ball, and handed it to Pia, who was still crying in Ellie's arms.

"Sorry," he said, once Ada had locked up and he and Ellie stood by her car. "I like playing catch, but I didn't know Pia would be such a huge fan."

"It's okay." Having fastened Pia's car seat latch, Ellie looked anything but okay.

"Anything else you need me to do?" He couldn't have said why, but intuition told him he was in the doghouse for something. "Grab milk? Bread?"

"Deacon, thank you, but everything's fine. I'm just tired after a long day. You must be, too."

He should be, but wasn't. More than anything, he wanted to follow Ellie and his daughter to their house. Cook dinner together, then veg on the couch. Nights spent playing video games or bar hopping with Garrett and Tristan held little appeal.

"Well, I need to get going." She shocked him with an ambush hug. "Thanks again for helping out."

THE WHOLE DRIVE HOME, Pia fitfully cried for her father.

Ellie tried soothing her by jiggling her feet at red lights, but her daughter wasn't having it. Could her mood be feeding off Ellie's own tension?

Why did it bother her so much that Pia seemed to have more and more fun with her dad? When Deacon walked into the store with Pia in his strong arms, Ellie had found it hard to breathe. His rough, tough masculinity combined with her baby girl's soft sweetness had been one heck of a powerful combination. For a split second, Ellie had felt inordinately blessed, as if life had delivered the ultimate do-over in placing Deacon in her life. Only he wasn't hers, but Pia's. Which Ellie truly believed was a wonderful gift for her little girl. So why was Ellie resentful of the fun they shared? Maybe because no matter how hard she tried ignoring her attraction for him, she couldn't. Because every time she did, that old longing for him that had resulted in the conception of their child returned to haunt her.

She remembered the feel of his skin against hers. The way she'd felt safe when he'd held her. Safe to do things—wild things—she'd ordinarily never consider. His kisses had been all-consuming, flooding her with dangerous heat....

The car behind her honked.

Just thinking about that night with Deacon had her missing green lights. What else was reuniting with him liable to do? But then, silly her, Deacon had shown no signs he'd like a friendship, and he hadn't crossed any lines indicating he craved a repeat performance of the wild night they'd once shared. Even if he had, that was the last thing *she* wanted. He'd been Tom's best friend, for heaven's sake.

Pia was still crying.

"I know, baby. I'm ready to get home, too. We're almost there." Turning onto their street, seeing the dark house, made her sad.

If she'd wanted, Deacon probably would've come over. Shared dinner and coffee, and helped her put Pia to bed. It was what might happen next that worried

Ellie. Would they watch a movie? Talk about shared
times with Tom? Plan for Pia's future?

All of that sounded pleasant on the surface, but Ellie
was terrified of allowing herself to get too close. She'd
already once lost herself physically to Deacon. The last
thing she wanted was to lose herself to him emotionally, as well.

Chapter Eight

"Deacon?" Ellie yawned into her phone a few nights later. "What time is it? Everything okay?"

"It's 0315. Sorry to call so early, but I wanted you to know I'm heading out for a while. I won't have another chance to talk."

Pulse racing, she bolted upright in her bed. "Th-thanks for letting me..." It was impossible to speak past a knot of dread. Just when Pia was growing more and more attached to him, he was leaving. What if something happened to him? How would Pia cope with losing two fathers?

How would I cope with losing two men?

Though she and Deacon weren't romantically involved, their lives were nonetheless entwined. Where did she start in explaining how much he'd come to mean to her?

"You know the drill."

Unable to speak, she nodded. Silly. He couldn't see her.

"I promised the peanut we'd see that new Disney movie Saturday. Think you can take her?"

"So you're sure you won't make it back by then?"

"Ell..." His tone said what she already knew from

her time with Tom. Deacon couldn't tell her a thing about where he was going or what he'd be doing.

"I understand. But we'll save the movie for when you're home safe." *Home*. Such a loaded word. Was this Deacon's home? The way she'd treated him, no. The way her heart ached at his leaving? Absolutely. But what did that mean? How did she begin making sense of feelings indecipherable even to herself?

"Dive! Dive!" Deacon's commanding officer shouted.

Despite gunfire barraging his team, the last thing Deacon wanted was to even momentarily retreat, but he did as he was told, easing under black water. Hanging at a depth of fifteen feet, they were safe from anything shot from the cargo ship's rail.

Though his dive mask was outfitted with night vision capabilities, the sensation of floating in darkness, hearing the muted cracked-whip sounds of bullets slicing the water, was an eerie experience. Deacon struggled to find his usual adrenaline rush. Instead of excitement charging his every move, something else drove him: a forbidden image of Ellie holding their little girl. He didn't want to see her. She belonged to Tom. But there it was, stuck in his head with no sign of letting him go.

"Roll call," said the commander over his radio.

One by one, members of Deacon's team called in. They were all safe. All ready to kick modern-day pirate ass.

Ten minutes later, the bad guys were either dead or cuffed.

The ship's captain and crew all talked at once, in at least twenty African dialects.

Job done, Deacon and the rest of his team turned over

the operation to a waiting navy crew. Just as stealthily as SEAL Team 12 had arrived on the scene, they now vanished.

Deacon had never been more happy to be headed home.

"YOU'RE BACK!" At ten on a Thursday night, the last person Ellie expected to stroll through her kitchen door was Deacon, but boy, was she glad to see him. Without stopping to think if she should, she ran from where she'd been doing dishes at the sink to crush him in a hug.

"Damn," he teased, holding her just as tightly, "if I'd known I'd get this warm of a welcome, maybe I should leave more often."

"Don't even think about it." She stepped back, delivering a light smack to his chest, but he held her hand over his heart. Like hers, it was pounding.

"How's our girl?"

"Sleeping. Finally. She missed you." Unable to bear touching him any longer, Ellie reclaimed her hand, holding it against her as if she might retain his warmth. But why? She'd always had a certain physical fascination with Deacon, but nothing like this. Guilt tightened her chest.

"I missed her."

And me?

Pressing her hands to her forehead, Ellie tried willing these ludicrous thoughts to stop. It happened. Widows crushing on their husband's best friends, not out of real attraction, but because of that shared connection. Surely, that's all this was?

Ellie trailed after Deacon to the nursery.

Standing before the crib, staring at their daughter,

he whispered, "Look at the ruffles on that cute little rump. New jammies?"

"Gift from nana and papa."

Curving his hand around Pia's curls, he said, "John and Helen have good taste."

In the hall, with the nursery door closed, Ellie asked, "Hungry? I roasted a chicken for dinner and there are plenty of leftovers."

"Sounds delicious, but let me help."

In under five minutes, they'd assembled a mini buffet on the counter. Ellie fiercely missed cooking for Tom—though just as often, he'd prepared meals for her. Maybe it was the sharing she missed most?

"Good Lord, this is delicious." At the table, eyes closed while chewing his second bite of mashed potatoes, Deacon looked exhausted, but content. "Now that I've been at this SEAL thing awhile, MREs taste worse every mission."

Ellie rose, going to a drawer she hadn't opened since Tom's last trip. It was filled with fast-food condiment packages. Every time she had any left over, she saved them for MRE seasoning. Cramming a Ziploc bag with everything from ketchup to Arby's sauce to mayonnaise, she gave it to Deacon. "Sorry I haven't been doing this for you all along. All the wives do. Not that you and I are…" She covered her face with her hands and she shook her head. "What's wrong with me? The whole time you've been gone I've been a wreck."

"Sorry." Deacon studied the pack. "But this will be greatly appreciated. You can't imagine how Garrett, Tristan and I envy the married guys for these."

"Good. I mean, that you like it. I'll start making them

for all three of you and the other single men, and just drop them at the base."

"That'd be nice."

Awkward didn't begin describing the silence hanging between them, yet the house wasn't particularly quiet. The evening news played on the living room TV. The newly fixed washer thumped away, doing a load of Pia's clothes. Ellie wanted to say so much to Deacon, but wasn't sure how to express her innermost thoughts. Or even why she felt the need. Forcing a breath, she blurted, "Can we start over?"

"What do you mean?" he asked in midbite.

"I guess you leaving reminded me that no matter how afraid I am of Tom's parents learning the truth about Pia, I'm even more terrified of Pia—" *and me* "—losing you."

Their eyes locked and Ellie's pulse took off at a runaway gallop. For the longest time, Deacon said nothing, but then he put down his fork and shocked her by taking her hand.

"The old me would've already been drinking at a bar, but the new me—Pia's dad—wants you to know I'm not going anywhere." He bowed his head. "Trouble is, we both know that's not entirely up to me to decide."

Unable to think with him touching her, Ellie nodded, but wasn't a hundred percent clear on what he'd even meant. Was he referring to his dangerous job? Or something deeper—that he perhaps cared so much for Pia that he wanted to stick around, but needed Ellie's permission?

"Baby, it's okay," Deacon crooned in the theater lobby Saturday afternoon. Pia had been traumatized by a pretty freakin' scary forest scene. What were those Disney people thinking? "Daddy's not going to let any of those talking rocks hurt you."

Or anything else, for that matter.

"Bad rocks," his little girl said with a sniffle, hiding her face in the crook of his neck.

"I know."

"Everything all right?" Ellie asked. Assuming this would be a quick fix, Deacon had left her inside, telling her he'd handle the situation. But calming Pia was taking longer than he'd expected.

"Getting there." A few more jiggles had the toddler at least grinning through her tears. "Looks like we might need to change our plans."

"Want to just go back to my place?" Ellie asked.

"No way." Tickling Pia's ribs, Deacon said, "Let's get revenge on some evil rocks."

Ten minutes later, he had buckled her into her safety seat and now sat beside Ellie, heading toward Cold Creek quarry. This was the first time he'd been with Ellie in Tom's Jeep. Cars were personal. This one held memories for her as surely as one of Tom's favorite sweaters.

"She's sleeping," Ellie said after a glance in the backseat.

"I feel bad."

"Why?"

"For even taking her." He upped the heat, aiming the vents toward Pia. "Bad parent move."

"How were you supposed to know? What are you going to do? Preview every movie she ever sees?"

"If that's what it takes to keep her smiling." Veering onto the highway, he ignored Ellie's stare.

"You do realize that's the dumbest thing you've ever said."

"Why? Just because you don't think it's always possible to keep Pia happy?"

Hands clasped on her thighs, Ellie looked as if she was done with the conversation. Unfortunately, she changed her mind. "Of all people, you should know you have a zero percent chance of controlling every instant of Pia's life. Movies are scary. Boys turn out to be jerks. Worse yet, they're princes who ultimately die."

"Way to ruin the day." Never had he wished more for a nice, cozy bottle of Patrón. It didn't talk back. And it sure as hell didn't tell him he was wrong.

"Nothing's ruined. I'm just keeping things real. You seem to have a fairy-tale view of parenting. Worse yet, a SEAL's view."

He tightened his grip on the wheel. "What's that supposed to mean? SEALs are awesome. There's *nothing* we can't do."

"My point exactly." Arms folded, lips pressed into a scowl, Ellie stared out her window. "Last I checked, y'all hadn't yet mastered immortality."

"You really wanna go there? For a woman claiming to want a fresh start between us, you have a damn funny way of showing it."

"Language," she snapped.

He veered onto their exit. "I'll be first to admit even SEALs can't learn new cuss words in their sleep. Doubt our daughter can, either."

"You make me crazy."

"Feeling's mutual, sweetheart."

AT THE SHALLOW END of the rock quarry Deacon had somehow known about, Ellie leaned against the car, arms folded.

Pia's delighted shrieks echoed across the lonely space. "Daddy fun! Do again!"

Deacon grabbed a huge rock and hurled it into the water where it landed with a great splash.

"Again!"

"No." He kept his voice gentle and calm and infinitely patient with their little girl. "Now it's your turn. You need to get those bad rocks and throw them in the water."

He handed her a small stone, guiding her arm to show her how to get the most distance.

When Pia succeeded, she jumped and giggled. "Bad rock!"

"That's right." Deacon handed her another. "You showed him not to be so mean."

"Bad, bad rock!" Pia had the hang of it, and was soon selecting her own rocks to punish.

The scene was unbearably sweet. Big, strong Deacon towering above little Pia. The sight should've filled Ellie with warmth. Instead, she wished herself home in bed so she could hide under the covers and cry.

Why couldn't this situation be easier? Why did Deacon and she share such a complicated past? If he hadn't been Tom's best friend, could she have allowed herself to fall for him?

It hadn't been that long ago when she'd asked him to let her tag along on his and Pia's fun outings. Here they all were, yet Ellie was the only one not having fun—not because of anything Deacon had done, but because of her own stupid inability to let go. Maybe she was afraid that if she enjoyed herself too much with him, she'd lose control? Not physically, but emotionally.

He was a great guy. Any woman would be thrilled to have him. But in her heart, Ellie was still taken.

Would always be taken.

Toss in the paternity issue and their relationship was a full-scale disaster.

"Mommy, look!" Pia held a rock so large she could hardly toss it in the water. "Me strong!"

"You sure are, baby!" Ellie's throat knotted.

"Bet you can't throw one that big," Deacon taunted.

"Watch me!" Ellie found the biggest rock she could and growled when she threw it. The resulting huge splash was her most satisfying accomplishment in a long time. "See?"

Kneeling next to their daughter, Deacon said to Pia, "I don't know, peanut. Think that was good enough for us to let Mommy attack rocks with us?"

The child answered with an enthusiastic nod. "Mommy fun!"

"If you say so…" Though Deacon was answering Pia, his eyes met Ellie's. The sheer weight of his stare turned her emotions topsy-turvy. The man was criminally handsome. "Can we start another truce?" he asked her.

Tears welling, she nodded.

He handed her a flat stone. "Time for a skip-off. Whoever skips the most with one throw has to make dinner."

"Oh, mister, you're on. We used to have a pond by our house and the neighbor kid taught me to skip like a champion." Ellie threw and with five skips was glad to see she hadn't lost her touch.

"Decent," he conceded, getting six on his first throw. "Tell me more about this neighbor kid. Any romance?"

"Maybe…" Ellie matched his six and found another stone she was sure could get seven. "You'll never know."

"Oh," he said with a laugh, getting only four on his latest throw, "I don't know about you, Pia, but that sounded like a challenge to me. Think Mommy needs tickling?"

"Tickle, tickle!" Laughing, the little girl was first to attack.

Then came Deacon, going straight for Ellie's vulnerable ribs.

Laughing so hard she could barely breathe, Ellie didn't fight it when they all collapsed onto the ground in a laughing, tickling pile.

"Mommy funny!" Pia announced, sitting on her father's chest.

"Me?" Ellie complained. "What about your dad? Isn't he funny?"

Pia nodded, then threw her chubby arms around both of them. "I love you."

"Love you, too, sweetie." Deacon kissed Pia's cheek, in the process making eye contact with Ellie. In that moment, the three of them felt like a family, and the sensation was intoxicating, exhilarating and more. Too bad the reality of their situation didn't match up.

Ellie kissed Pia's other cheek, and for the longest time they lay there breathing heavily in the foggy air.

"You do know I let you win?" Deacon stood at the stove making a stir-fry he'd concocted from veggies he'd found in Ellie's fridge, and frozen round steak he'd defrosted, then cut into strips.

"Right." The queen of rock throwing, who'd somehow managed to skip a stone nine times, sat comfy-cozy in an armchair, her legs covered by a warm throw. With her dark hair a mess and her cheeks still rosy from the cold, she looked too pretty. The kind of pretty that could drive a man into begging to be domesticated. "Just keep dreaming."

Pia had conked out on the sofa, watching a cartoon movie with no killer rocks, and the foggy mist had changed to a drizzle, then snow.

Tossing in diced garlic, Deacon said, "Tell me more about this neighbor kid who supposedly taught you all you know. How old were you and was there necking involved?"

Ellie's snorting laugh did funny things to his chest. Mostly, it made him want to make her laugh more. "God's honest truth, he was the cutest boy I'd ever seen, and when he kissed me behind the lawnmower shed, that's the closest I've ever come to swooning."

"Damn... Tom know about all this?"

"Yes, but he made me promise to never go behind the lawnmower shed again." Turning thoughtful, she added, "Easy enough, since the last time I visited my mom it looked ready to collapse."

"How often do you see her?" He added a cup of rice to boiling water.

Ellie groaned. "Probably not enough, but I tried near Halloween and it went bad. I thought the visit was going all right, but then she asked if she could borrow a twenty for bread. Since her eyes were glassy and there was a full loaf on the counter, I'm guessing her dealer was getting my money and not the nearest grocery store. Once I left home, she moved on to mostly drugs."

"Ouch." After stirring the rice, he added a lid to the pan. "Sorry."

"How about you? Have any special family memories you'd like to share?"

"Fresh out. I guess there's a part of me that wouldn't mind seeing my mom." As for his dad? That reunion would never happen.

FOR ELLIE, life would actually be pleasant if only her new family of three could remain indefinitely in this holding pattern. But she knew what expectations Deacon had for her to share their truth, and the days until she made good on her promise were ticking away.

By the night Ellie bundled up Pia for her preschool's Thanksgiving program, Deacon had become a welcome addition to both their lives. In the play, Pia's role was a turkey. It'd taken Deacon six hours Monday night to get all her feathers just right. He was supposed to be meeting them at the school, and no matter how hard she fought to deny it, Ellie looked forward to seeing him. To being on the receiving end of his smile. To watching him interact with their daughter.

The school, filled to the rafters with running, laughing preschoolers and their doting families, had been decorated in a full-on Pilgrim theme complete with cornucopia cutouts and cornstalks and the scent of dozens of pumpkin pies.

"Where's Daddy?" Pia asked.

"He'll be here soon." *I hope.*

Ellie tried holding on to her daughter, but once she found her teacher and a group of friends, she tottered off, giggling and holding hands. Ellie made small talk with a few moms, but what she most wanted was to see Deacon strolling down the crowded hall.

By the time the principal announced the program's start, Deacon still hadn't arrived.

Ellie should've been disappointed for Pia, but in reality, she was the one who'd spent extra time with her hair and makeup, and changed clothes three times before finding just the right sweater, jean and boot combo.

Casting one last glance over her shoulder before entering the auditorium, she saw him.

Pulse racing, she felt voyeuristic watching him remove his leather jacket and gloves. His hair had grown out again, and was a dark mess. His square jaw sported a day's growth. He still wore black cargo pants, boots and a T-shirt, and every woman present had eyes on him. The fact that he chose to make a beeline for Ellie turned her stomach into a somersault festival.

"Hey, gorgeous." Casually clasping her waist, he bent to deliver a platonic kiss to her cheek. Why was she wishing for more?

"Hey, yourself. Glad you could come."

"Looked dicey for a bit, but considering the fancy hair you're sporting, it was worth the effort to make it through my workout in half the usual time."

He'd noticed. Was it wrong that her spirits soared as if she were a giddy teen? "Stop. My hair always looks like this."

He snorted. "I don't know what mirror you've been looking in, but I've never seen you this hot. Well…" He whispered in her right ear, his warm breath giving her shivers. "Unless we count that time a while back…" When she reddened, he had the good grace to look away and clear his throat. "But we probably shouldn't discuss that here."

Cheeks flaming, she elbowed him before leading the way to front seats.

"Did Pia's feathers stay on?" He folded his coat over the back of the chair.

"Beautifully. You did a great job. I never would've thought of using that chopped up red rubber ball for the head and wattle. Her costume beat every other kid's."

"Awesome."

Laughing, Ellie covered her face with her hands. "Our daughter is barely two and already we're obsessing over her being the best. What does that say about what we'll be like when she's ten?"

A funny look crossed his face. One Ellie couldn't begin to decipher. Taking her hand, he eased his fingers between hers, upping her pulse by a couple hundred percent. "What it says is that we're going to be amazing—and so is Pia."

At that moment, in the auditorium's dim light and balmy heat, Ellie believed him. When he squeezed her hand, she squeezed back, her gaze never leaving his. Her usual guilt was there, but so was something else she hadn't felt in a really long time—anticipation for what might come next.

Chapter Nine

She's mine. That adorable dancing turkey outsinging all her friends by at least three decibels was his child. Deacon's chest ached with pride. Had his parents ever felt this way about him? Or only his brother? Where in their raising of two children had they made a conscious decision to love only one? Or had his less than perfect teen years been more a reflection of his poor behavior rather than his parents?

"Ell?" he whispered during a scene where Pia stood in the back with a few dancing potatoes. "Do you think I should call my dad?"

"That's random," she whispered back. "What made you think of him?"

Pia skipped to the front of the stage.

"Never mind. We'll talk about it after the show."

Hand on his forearm, she nodded.

After the performance, after slivers of pumpkin pie that left them wanting more, after he and Ellie shared one side of a booth at a local diner because Pia was asleep on the other, Deacon once again got around to bringing up his parents. "Remember earlier, when I asked you about my dad?"

She nodded.

Swirling the coffee they'd ordered while waiting for pie, Deacon struggled to compose his thoughts. "Watching my own child brought on an epiphany. Hell, if I'm even using the right word."

"Like an *aha* moment?" She added cream and sugar to her coffee.

"Exactly." He liked that she got it. "Anyway, I was sitting there watching her, and wondered what I could've possibly done that was bad enough for my parents not to love me."

Eyes watering, Ellie didn't say anything, just eased her arm around his shoulders.

"For years, I've shied from any commitments—at least to anything other than the navy. But tonight, it occurred to me that my dad had a choice. All along, he'd had the free will to decide to put my big brother first. That wasn't my fault, you know? And it sure as hell has nothing to do with the way I—we—choose to raise Pia. As for me avoiding long-term relationships like the plague..." He laughed, then sipped his coffee. "Again, that's the old fear in me talking. The part of me afraid I'd never be loved. But tonight..." his throat tightened "...tonight, when I looked at our little girl, my heart felt impossibly full. I didn't know I was capable of loving so deeply, but I am—and that shocked me. And made me happy at the same time. And it made me wonder if I've been wrong about other things, too." *Like whether or not I could sustain a relationship with a woman.* But that opened a whole new can of worms, because it wasn't just *any* woman who held him spellbound, but his dead best friend's wife. What was wrong with him?

"I don't know." She swallowed hard. "You asked if I

thought you should call your dad. If you think there's a chance for a reconciliation, I say go for it, but—"

"No, not for a second do I believe he'll ever stop blaming me for Peter's death. But I know I had nothing to do with it, and that's enough for me. Guess part of me wanted him to know I'm a father now, and that no matter what he thinks of me, I'm going to be all right."

Ellie's misty-eyed smile warmed him through and through. "For the life of me, I can't see how Pia's turkey dance dredged all this up for you, but whatever vanquishes past demons is always good. I guess there is one thing bugging me, though…"

"What?" He finished his coffee.

"Forgive me if I'm out of line with this, but sounds like your main objective in calling your dad would be to thumb your nose at him. But, Deacon, you're better than that. And the truth is, don't you think he knows not only what a success you've made of your life, but that it was in spite of him, rather than because of him?"

Their pie arrived—pumpkin for him and banana cream for Ellie. After the waitress refilled their coffee cups and left, he admitted, "I hadn't thought of it that way. Guess for so many years I've been pissed off, it never occurred to me he did me a favor. Pure rage got me through BUD/S. But tonight, watching Pia—" he grinned "—it's gone. Replaced by what I'm pretty sure is this weird thing in the pit of my stomach… Maybe I'm happy?"

Laughing, Ellie pulled him into another hug, followed by a kiss to his nose and then cheek. A fraction of an inch from landing her mouth on his lips, she drew back and cleared her throat. "Not sure what's wrong

with you," she whispered, "but I suspect you're con-
tagious."

"You're happy, too?" he teased, shamefully wishing
she'd gone for that kiss.

"Think so." She forked a piece of her pie. "Trouble
is, how do I give myself permission? With Tom gone,
I can't seem to reconcile the guilt."

THANKSGIVING DAY, Ellie set her prettiest table, cooked
to the point of exhaustion then tried squelching the fear
knotting her gut. Helen and John would be here any
moment. Garrett and his latest girl had already arrived,
and watched a parade with Pia and Ada. Tristan had
gone south to celebrate with his mother. Though Deacon had been a great help to her in the kitchen, he'd
also been tense, wondering whether or not to call his
parents. Ellie told him to at least phone his mom, then
see what unfolded. He talked to her for five minutes in
awkward, choppy sentences, hanging up without having really said anything at all.

"Smells wonderful." Sneaking up behind her at the
stove, he stole a green bean.

"Stop!" She pushed him away. "What if Helen and
John show up early? They shouldn't see you looking
so comfortable."

"Wow." He took a roll from a basket on the counter
and tossed it from one hand to his other. "If you ask
me, you'd feel a lot better getting this paternity issue—
along with our friendship—out in the open."

"That's probably true, but not entirely your decision." When it came to the information she had to let
Helen and John know, Ellie would be the first to admit
she was a coward.

"Relax." Deacon pulled her into a hug she guiltily enjoyed. "For the moment, your secret's safe with me."

Despite his reassurance, when the doorbell rang, Ellie leaped away from Deacon, stirring gravy while striving for a look of normalcy.

"You gonna get that?" he asked.

"Could you? Please?" Quivery from the realization that if her in-laws hadn't announced their arrival, she'd have been caught in Deacon's arms, Ellie was instantly transformed from competent cook to weak-kneed widow just trying to make it through the day.

In the end, she heard Garrett and Ada sharing small talk with Tom's folks, volunteering to take their coats.

Though Deacon hopefully hadn't noticed, she'd been up since five, not just basting the turkey, but clearing the public parts of the house of his personal things. Helen wouldn't understand why his favorite hat or magazines or even socks had found themselves a home in Tom's house.

Why do you care?

Ellie cared because the little girl inside her who'd struggled her whole life to be loved and accepted finally felt as if she belonged to a real family. The rational part of her pointed out that that's exactly what Deacon and Pia and she were well on their way to becoming. Why couldn't all of them just live in harmony? Why did she have to lose Deacon to keep Helen and John?

"There's our other pretty girl." With Pia already settled on her hip, sporting a new tiara Ellie hadn't before seen, Helen crossed the kitchen to give her a one-arm hug. "Mmm, as wonderful as it smells in here, we should've brought you a crown, too."

"Thanks, but I'm good," Ellie said with a forced laugh.

"You all right?" Helen pressed the back of her hand to Ellie's forehead. "Hope you're not coming down with something. We just heard at church that an early flu is already going around."

"I'm fine," Ellie assured her. "Just tired."

"What can Pia and I do to help?"

"I made a Jell-O salad. Mind taking it out of the mold? The serving platter's next to the toaster."

"Want to help Mommy?" Helen asked her granddaughter.

Pia nodded. "Daddy help, too."

On her way to the fridge, Helen winced. "That's still going on? Pia thinking of Deacon as her father?"

Tell her! the voice of reason in Ellie's head screamed. She would never have a more perfect segue. Not only did her conscience demand that she finally get the whole truth out in the open, but so did her growing loyalty to Deacon. He'd been there for her and Pia lately more times than she could count. He didn't just deserve to be publically known as Pia's dad, but he'd earned the right by being as good a father as any little girl had ever had. Certainly better than what Ellie had experienced.

Better than Tom?

Her conscience asked an unfair question.

Tom would've been an amazing father to Pia in every way, but for whatever reason, he'd been taken from them prematurely. As Pia's mom, the duty to continue their little girl's care fell square on Ellie's shoulders. No matter how conflicted she might be about her attraction for Deacon, there was no question his being an integral part of Pia's life was a very good thing.

"Helen." Ellie clasped her hands. "I'm not trying to start anything, but why do you seem threatened by Deacon? He was Tom's best friend. He's my friend. What does his being with Pia hurt? She adores him."

Helen had taken the Jell-O from the fridge and now filled the sink with warm water. Before speaking, she glanced over her shoulder. Making sure she and Ellie were the only adults listening? "I like Deacon. Tom liked him, but also worried. According to our son, Deacon drinks too much, drives too fast and goes through women more quickly than days on a calendar. Tom once said he trusted him implicitly in battle, but…" Helen's eyes filled with tears. She turned off the faucet and set the metal turkey mold into the water. "We all know how Tom's last mission went."

"You blame Deacon for Tom's death?" Bile rose in Ellie's throat. Deacon had already carried the incalculable burden of his brother's death for far too long. No way should he also carry the weight of Tom's passing. "Helen, Tom was everything to me, and if I thought for one second Deacon had played any role in his death, I would move heaven and earth to see my husband avenged. But Tom was a soldier. He played very dangerous games and came out on the losing end. How could Deacon have controlled what I've been told was a sniper's shot?"

"There must have been something…" Helen removed the mold from the water, running a knife around the edges before topping it with the platter. She turned it over and gave the pan a light shake. The Jell-O snapped out far more perfectly than it ever had for Ellie. Was that a sign? That just as Helen was older and wiser and

better at salad molds, she was also right about Deacon?
"Something Deacon could've done."

"No. Helen, you know I love you like you're my own
mother, but on this, you're wrong."

"Nana." Pia looked up at Helen, holding her favorite
doll, Miss Sparkles, whose dress had come undone. She
also had a tiny plastic doll no bigger than a quarter that
one of the kids from preschool had given her. Ellie had
taken it on a couple of occasions, but her little monkey
must've plucked it from the trash. "Fix button?"

"Of course, honey." Turning to Ellie, she asked,
"Where do you keep your sewing kit?"

Ellie told her. While Pia was distracted, Ellie took the
miniature doll and set it on the counter. It was a relief
once again having the kitchen to herself. She didn't need
minutes to process Helen's words, more like weeks.
Were they just rantings from a bitter mother who'd lost
her only son? Or more? True, immediately after Tom's
death, Deacon had been drunk and reckless and rude,
but that wasn't him anymore. He was a changed man,
and Ellie believed his relationship with Pia, his desire
to become a great dad, had everything in the world to
do with his positive life changes.

*What about me? Could I have in some small way
stopped him from chasing his own demons?*

"How's it going?" When Deacon appeared behind
her, standing close enough for her to feel his heat, she
flinched. "You're jumpy. Everything okay?"

"Um, sure." Nothing could be further from the truth.

"Can I help?"

"No, thank you." *Yes! Help me figure out whose side
I'm on.* Since she'd lost Tom, Deacon had become her
proverbial knight in shining armor. How could some-

one she also depended upon, like Helen, hold such a completely different opinion of the same man? "I think we're ready to eat."

"Sure smells good." John sauntered into the room, bearing a breezy smile and a bottle of white wine. "Helen says white meat calls for white wine, and as we all know," he said with a wink, "she usually knows best."

UPON CLOSING THE DOOR behind their last guest, Deacon leaned against it and sighed. God only knew how much he loved his daughter, but the whole extended family routine had him craving his old friend Patrón.

Despite the crackling fire's dancing glow, the rich scents of turkey and pumpkin and cranberries still flavoring the air, and Harry Connick Jr. doing his mellow thing on the stereo, Deacon couldn't help but feel tense.

"Long day, huh?" Ellie cleared what few dessert plates and utensils were still on the dining room table, carrying them to the kitchen sink.

Deacon followed.

Pia had long since crashed on the living room sofa.

"Endless. Was it just me, or was there a bad vibe between you and Helen?"

Ellie leaned her elbows on the counter, covering her face with her hands.

Deacon went to her, lightly massaging the base of her neck. "Judging by how tight you are, I must've missed something fairly major. Did you tell her about Pia?"

Ellie shook her head.

"Then what?"

"I don't want to tell you." Her voice barely rose above the music.

Deacon's stomach clenched. "That's all the more reason for me to know."

"No. It's too painful."

After a sharp exhalation, he arched his head back and stepped away. What the hell had Helen said? He also had a fondness for her, but maybe he'd been too quick to judge her a friend. "Tell me or I'm leaving."

"Where are you going to go? Gonna hit your favorite bar? Be reckless with your bike? You've done enough running, Deacon." Ellie eased her arms around his waist, resting her head against his heart. His pulse always quickened when she was near, but this time was different. Somehow she'd become his safe harbor. The fact that she would keep a secret from him rubbed him raw.

"Tell me."

"Helen blames you for Tom's death. There, I said it. Feel better?" Grabbing a box of Saran Wrap, Ellie drew a piece out, slapping it over the remaining pumpkin pie.

Deacon wasn't sure what he'd expected her to say. Anything but that.

"Deacon, I understand how—"

"You understand? No. I've been blamed for one death in my life and that was enough. Losing my brother changed my life's course. Seeing the look on my father's face made me wish I'd died instead of Peter. The navy saved me. Tom's friendship saved me." Grabbing Ellie's upper arms, Deacon said, "You have to believe I did everything I could to keep him with us, but God had other plans."

Clutching the front of his shirt, she pulled him toward her. Time froze when again they stopped perilously short of sharing a kiss. "I fought for you right to her face. That's why we were at odds all day, because I told her she was wrong." Tears streamed down Ellie's cheeks. "She has you all wrong."

"Does she?" To know Ellie believed in him meant more than she could ever know. He held on to her for all he was worth. "I've replayed Tom's death a million times in my head. I know in my heart that other than me taking the bullet for him by standing where he'd been, there was nothing I could do. I tried stopping the blood, but it came too fast." He buried his head in Ellie's sweet, flowery hair. It was soft and so foreign from that hot, dark corner of the world where Tom had died that all Deacon wanted to do was lose himself in this woman's beautiful smell.

"I know…." She reached up, caressed his face. "Let's leave this mess till morning. Everything looks better with sunshine."

"Sure. You go on to bed."

"I think you misunderstood." Taking his hand, she kissed his palm. "The last thing I want is to be alone. I don't want you to be alone, either."

"I'm not prepared to—well, you know what, Ell. Not like this."

"Did I ask you to? What's wrong with holding each other? Is it wrong for me to want to be held?"

Chapter Ten

Ellie woke in Deacon's arms. Even though they'd slept till seven-thirty, the room was dark. Sleet clawed the windows.

Despite the ugly weather, Ellie snuggled closer to Deacon. He was so warm, and after yesterday, a bone-deep chill had taken hold. Her world felt upside down. She loved Helen. Ellie wasn't yet sure what she felt for Deacon, but whatever it was, she needed him in her life.

The last man she'd shared this bed with had been Tom, but her life with him seemed a million miles away. And for once, that was okay. She would always love him, but that love had changed. Softened into a beautiful memory she'd forever cherish.

From behind her, she heard a sleepy groan. She closed her eyes in pleasure to feel Deacon's warm breath, then a kiss on the nape of her neck. "Good morning."

"Yes, it is." Relaxed against him, Ellie felt as if the bed had become an island in the midst of her life's wreckage. Before yesterday, she'd placed Helen high on a pedestal. Now, her mother-in-law had been reduced to mere mortal status, which made Ellie sad, but also a lot more mature. No one was perfect. Yet everyone deserved forgiveness for their mistakes. Ellie had already forgiven Helen, but would her mother-in-law be kind enough to do the same?

Squeezing her tighter, Deacon said, "Remember how we promised the peanut a trip to the mall to see Santa today?"

Now Ellie was the one groaning. "With any luck, she forgot. What were we thinking? The day after Thanksgiving should be spent lounging in front of a fire eating leftovers, not fighting mall traffic."

"Agreed, but I'm not going to be the one breaking her heart. You tell her."

"What am I supposed to say?" Tracing her finger down his forearm, Ellie suggested, "Santa is really a SEAL and he had to leave town on a mission?"

Deacon laughed. "That's actually pretty good. Only a SEAL could easily accomplish all the big guy does in one night."

That cocky statement earned him a smack.

"Santa!" Dressed in the footy pajamas they'd changed her into before tucking her in the night before, Pia crawled onto the bed, then proceeded to jump. "Santa! Santa!"

Deacon sat up, pulling his daughter onto his lap to blow a raspberry on her cheek. "I can't wait to see Santa! But I think your mom has bad news."

"You're a rat," Ellie exclaimed. Obviously, without major tears, there was no way they'd be able to skip this outing. "But since the mall doesn't open till ten, let's at least go out for a nice, civilized breakfast."

"Hate to break this to you," Deacon said, looking extra adorable with their daughter on his lap, "but I just saw an ad on TV that the mall is open at 6:00 a.m.

for the whole holiday season. We could be taking pics with Santa *right now*." He winked.

"Now, Santa! Now!" Pia leaped to her feet and resumed bouncing.

"You and I," Ellie said to Deacon, "are no longer friends. Have you looked outside?"

"What's a little sleet? Maybe if we're really lucky it'll turn to snow."

Oh, it snowed all right. By the time they left the mall, laden with gifts for everyone from Helen and John to Garrett and Tristan to Ada, the parking lot was covered in at least six inches.

The line to see Santa in his workshop had wound all the way from the Jelly Belly Hut to Sears, the equivalent of twenty miles in mall walking.

Through it all, Deacon hadn't just kept his cool, but he'd schlepped heavy bags and even Pia when she grew fussy in her stroller.

Almost to the car, a familiar voice called, "Deacon? Is that you?"

Ellie turned to see the base commander's wife, Paula, jogging toward them through still-falling snow.

"Hey, Mrs. Duncan." Deacon raised the hand holding the fewest bags in a wave.

"I run into you at the oddest places—and Ellie and Pia. I think of you often. How are you?"

"We're good." Though the woman's voice was friendly, Ellie got the feeling she was also fishing for information on whether or not they were an item. Navy wives, Ellie supposed, were just like many others—they loved to gossip. "Thanks for asking."

"Finish your shopping?" she asked.

"Mostly," Ellie said. "We still have a few to go for certain little people." She grinned and nodded Pia's way.

"Ah, she's a cutie." Mrs. Duncan tugged one of the swinging pom-poms on Pia's hat. "I haven't even started on my grandkids. With six, it takes me days. William never does a thing to help. You're lucky to have wrangled Deacon into at least being your pack mule."

"I am." Ellie nodded, glancing his way. There he stood, snow piling on his shoulders, carrying at least fifty pounds of stuff without showing the slightest strain. The entire day he'd been good-natured and generous and helpful. And handsome. And funny. And a wonderful, wonderful father to Pia. "I am very lucky."

"Well, guess I'd better get all of this in my trunk. Bought my daughter a way-too-pricey leather purse that probably shouldn't get wet."

"Need help?" Deacon asked.

"No," she said with a laugh, "but you're a sweet boy for asking. You kids enjoy the rest of your night."

Once Pia was safely clicked into her seat and Deacon pulled the car out of the lot to join the long line of others fighting their way from the mall, he said, "Did you mean that?"

"What?" His profile was lit by the dash lights, and the sight of him quickened Ellie's breath.

"That line you told my commander's wife. About you being lucky—you know, for having me in your life. Is that true?"

She took his hand and smiled. "More than you'll ever know."

"Snow the day after Thanksgiving and sunny and sixty on Christmas. Methinks Mother Nature is confused."

Deacon stepped back from the living room's French doors. "Should we wake the peanut to get a jump start on opening her gifts?"

"What's your hurry?" Ellie yawned. She looked so pretty curled into a corner of the sofa, hugging a throw pillow, her long hair a tousled mess. The affection he felt for her was almost painful. Like if he lost her or Pia, he wasn't sure what he'd do.

"Helen and John aren't due until five for dinner," Ellie added. "They wanted to be with Pia Christmas morning, but I couldn't take the pressure."

"Of us all being together?" If his plan worked, Ellie wouldn't have to worry anymore.

"Santa?" Pia rounded the hall corner, rubbing sleepy eyes. "He came! He came!"

Pia jumped onto her hot pink big-girl bike with training wheels. Deacon had spent most of the night assembling it, but all traces of his exhaustion vanished upon seeing his daughter smile.

"Pretty!" Glitter handlebars with streamers were accompanied by a sparkly pink seat. "Ride! Ride!"

Since it was such a nice day, Deacon opened the deck doors, letting her circle around. The air smelled sweet, with the far-off promise of spring.

"While Pia's playing, how about you open a present?" Deacon reached into the thigh pocket of his camo pants, withdrawing a small box.

"Deacon..." Ellie's pale blue nightgown fluttered about her calves in the light breeze. The filmy fabric was translucent, only bettering the view. Sweeping flyaway hair behind her ears, she asked, "What did you do?"

"Vroom! Vroom!"

On bended knee, with their daughter happily circling, Deacon said, "I know I should wait for a more romantic moment and you don't have to say yes right away—or forever, I guess. But the truth is, we share a beautiful daughter, and even though part of me feels traitorous to Tom, he's not here and we are. I know we still have a ways to go before we're even a real couple, but more than anything, Ell, I want us to try. I want you, me and Pia to always be together, and—"

"Deacon...I don't know what to say. This is so sudden."

"What are you talking about? You have to have felt whatever it is growing between us."

"Vrooom!"

"Of course, but..." Tears filled her eyes. "You know how much you mean to me, but I'm afraid."

"Of what? You have to agree that lately life's been good."

She nodded and sniffled.

He took out the simple, square-cut ring a jeweler had assured him she'd love, and slipped it on her ring finger. "Look, it's a perfect fit. Isn't that a sign?"

"It is really pretty."

Damn straight. Took him and Pia a good hour to pick, not that their antsy little girl had been much help. "Like I said, this isn't something we have to jump into right away. I'm just tired of you and me being in limbo. I want—*need*—for you and Pia to officially be mine."

Nodding, she agreed.

Relieved beyond words, Deacon settled into the spirit of Christmas morning. Hoping, praying phase II of his plans for the day went just as well.

"Helen, Tom..." Ellie opened the front door, surprised to see her in-laws five hours early. She hadn't even had a shower yet, let alone started the ham and all the trimmings. "You're early."

"Deacon told us noon." Helen brushed past with an armload of gifts.

"Nana, Papa! I got bike!" Pia had gotten plenty of other gifts, too, but she was now seated on her bicycle, playing with two new dolls in the basket. "Look at me!"

"I see," Helen said on her way to place the presents under the tree. "You look so grown-up and pretty. I love all the sparkles."

"Me, too!"

"Ho, ho, ho!" John hefted two trash bags filled with more gifts. "Look what Santa left for you at our house, Miss Pia."

"Presents!" She hopped off her bike and skipped to the fragrant, decorated tree.

"Why did you tell them noon?" Ellie asked Deacon under her breath in the entry hall. "You knew we were having *dinner,* not lunch."

"It's all good. You'll see. I'll help you cook."

Ellie prayed his kiss to her forehead hadn't been noticed.

"Vrooom!" Pia was back to riding her bike, only now through the living room.

"How about this great weather?" John asked. "Whoa—sorry, I, uh, didn't mean to walk in on anything."

"That's okay." Much to her everlasting horror, Deacon slipped his hand around Ellie's waist, cinching her close. "I suppose now's as good a time as any to share our great news." Grabbing her left wrist, he held up her hand just in time for Tom's mother to enter the room. "Helen, John, this morning I asked Ell to marry me and she agreed."

Helen's complexion turned gray. "You can't be serious! Ellie, honey, please tell me this is a joke. You and I just talked. You know what kind of man Deacon is."

"Are you kidding me?" Deacon dropped his arm from Ellie's waist. "Ell told me you blame me for Tom's death, and that's total B.S."

"You going to allow him to talk like that in front of your daughter?" Helen asked Ellie. "Our granddaughter?"

"Ellie," John said, "you clearly aren't thinking straight. Deacon, man to man, while I appreciate all you've done for my son's wife and daughter, your services are no longer needed. Ellie…" Her father-in-law put his arm around her. "I'm sorry. Helen and I should've made this offer sooner, but you and Pia should come stay with us. You've been overwhelmed, but from here on out, we'll take care of everything."

"Please, all of you hush." Ellie pressed the heels of her hands against her forehead. Time for damage control. As long as Deacon kept his big mouth shut about Pia, everything would be okay. "Pia, honey, go play with your toys in your room."

"No!" She folded her arms. "Ride bike!"

"Her new ugly side is your influence," Helen said to Deacon.

"Come on," Ellie said to her little girl, "go ride on the deck."

"Vroom! Vroom!"

With her daughter just outside, but where she could still see her, Ellie looked to John. "I appreciate your more than kind offer, but I'm a grown woman and perfectly capable of living on my own."

"Then why is he always here?" Helen pointed to Deacon.

Deacon sighed. "For the love of God, Ell, I tried doing this your way. I wanted Tom's folks here early, so we'd have plenty of time for them to adjust to our news. I know how scared you've been, carrying this burden, so I thought why not help you out?"

Don't you do it, Deacon....

"You know," he continued, "give you a nudge."

"The only thing she needs help with," Helen said, "is getting you out of here. You've been honing in on our son's wife and child ever since he died. If you ask me, it looks suspicious."

"Helen," John scolded. "It's been over a year..."

"Oh, you wanna go there, Helen?" Deacon's expression had reverted back in time to full-on bad boy. "Here's the truth Ellie couldn't bear to tell you."

"Deacon, no!" she pleaded, gripping his shirt.

"Ell, sorry, but it's long past time for this secret to come out."

"What's he talking about, Ellie?" John asked. "Is Deacon holding something over you concerning our son?"

"Dammit!" Deacon snapped. "What did I ever do to you people but love your son? Yes, he died beside me, but a lot of other guys have, too. Their parents didn't have the audacity to blame me for something the devil with a sniper rifle did. As for the reason I've been over here as often as possible, Ellie, you want to tell them or should I?"

"Oh, God..." Covered with a cold sweat, her pulse racing to a dangerous degree, Ellie bolted for the bathroom. "I'm going to be sick."

Helen chased after her, banging on the closed door. "Ellie, honey? Are you okay? Let me in."

"Should I call the police?" John asked, his voice muted from where he no doubt stood alongside his wife.

Ellie emptied her stomach, then stood before the sink, pressing a cold rag to her flaming cheeks. This was all too much, and not the way she'd wanted her in-laws to learn the truth. Bracing herself, she cursed Deacon for forcing her into a corner where she had no choice but to fight.

Opening the door, she eyed three of the four people she loved most. "Helen, John, I don't know any other way to do this, so I'm going to come right out and say it. I—I'm sorry, so deeply sorry, but P-Pia isn't Tom's daughter, but Deacon's."

Chapter Eleven

For over four months, Deacon had believed this was what he wanted—for everyone, especially Tom's folks, to learn he was Pia's father. But now, seeing Helen on her knees, crying uncontrollably, with John behind her, trying to keep cool, but not looking much better, Deacon was ashamed.

"Look," he said, "I'm sorry everything came out this way. I just thought it was high time we all knew the truth."

"Take this." Ellie wrenched his ring from her finger, slapping it into his hand. "And get out. You're not the man I thought you to be."

"You can't be serious, can you?" He half laughed. "Ell, you had to tell them eventually. They had to know."

"Not like this, Deacon. It didn't have to be this way." Crouching next to Helen, Ellie pulled her into a hug. "I'm so sorry. You have to know there was never anything between Deacon and me when I was with your son. When Tom was alive, he was the only man for me. He was my world. Deacon and I shared one night before Tom and I even met. Deacon introduced me to Tom."

"D-did my son know?" John asked.

"No." Ellie was crying now, too. "I wish he had. I

tried several times to tell him, but like with you two, the timing didn't seem right. I love you. Pia loves you. In my heart, this changes nothing."

"How can you say that?" Helen tore herself away. "You let our son believe he fathered a child who wasn't his. You're not the woman I've always believed you to be."

"Helen, please," John warned. "Don't say things you'll later regret. Listen to Ellie, hon. Pia is still ours. She believes we're her grandparents and I believe Tom would always want us to be."

Deacon felt as if he were watching the scene unfold on a movie screen. Ellie and her in-laws would eventually rebuild trust and once again be a tight unit, but what about him? Why, when happiness was just within reach, had everything been ripped away?

Backing silently from the hall, he retreated to the deck, checking on his little girl.

"Hey, peanut," he said in a husky voice. He sat on the stairs leading to the yard. "Having fun?"

She hopped off her bike, ponytail flopping, crossing the wood planks with her funny, lopsided run. Wrapping her arms around his neck, she gave him a great hug. "I love you! Santa came!"

"I—I know."

"I *love* Santa!"

The French door creaked open and Ellie stepped out. Eyes red and cheeks tearstained, she asked, "Why are you still here?"

"Ell, please…" He held out her ring. "I'm begging you. Don't do this. I'm sorry for spilling things like I did, but you have to know it was for your own good. You never would've found the strength or the right time—"

"Get out of my house."

"After all we've shared? This is how you want to play it?"

Refusing to even make eye contact with him, she said, "Please, for Pia—*for me*—don't make any more of a scene."

"NANA PLAY?" Pia offered one of her dolls.

Ellie's heart shattered, seeing poor Helen look ten years beyond her age and exhausted. She sat in one of the kitchen armchairs, nursing a hot tea while Ellie and John worked on an early makeshift Christmas dinner.

"I'm sorry, sweetheart, but Nana doesn't feel like playing."

"Sick?" Just like she'd seen her mom do a hundred times over, Pia held her tiny hand to Helen's forehead to check for fever.

"No, but I could use a hug."

The little girl climbed onto her lap for a nice, long cuddle.

John asked Ellie, "These potatoes seem done to you?"

She stabbed a fork into one. "Yes. I'll get started on mashing them."

With Helen and Pia occupied, he put his hand on Ellie's back. "I'm not going to lie. What you told us comes as quite a shock. But you don't know how much I appreciate you allowing us to keep Pia in our lives. And I believe you, that when you were with Tom you never had eyes for anyone but him."

Turning off the burner, Ellie drained the potatoes. "I—I can't apologize enough for keeping this from you for so long. Pia and I both love you. I never meant to cause you or Helen pain."

They shared a hug, and Ellie wanted to believe it was a start to healing. But Helen had yet to speak to anyone but her husband or Pia.

Fury didn't begin describing what Ellie felt toward Deacon. Knowing him, his wish to be in control, she believed his explanation that he'd thought he was helping. But nothing could be further from the truth.

"Haven't seen you in a while," Maggie called from behind Tipsea's bar. "Garrett and Tristan told me today was the day you were going to pop the question to your baby's momma. Hope you being here instead of with her and your little girl isn't a bad sign."

"How about you pour me a double of Patrón and then ask."

She rounded the bar to give him a hug.

A sad Christmas song played on the jukebox and the smoky bar was filled mostly with single guys. A few couples were present. One of which slow-danced with a sweetness that made Deacon crave holding Ellie. He should've known the happiness he'd shared with Pia and her mom had been too good to be true.

"She turned you down?" Maggie asked, taking the stool beside him.

"Worse. Said yes, wore my ring for all of a few hours, then handed it back, hollering for me to get out of her house."

Maggie winced. "No wonder you need a drink. This have anything to do with the in-laws finding out about you being Pia's daddy?"

"Yep."

Rubbing his back and making sympathetic clucking sounds, she shook her head. "Women. Can't live with 'em, can't make 'em listen to reason."

"No truer words were ever spoken." He tapped the bar. "Not to change the subject, but what's a guy gotta do to get a drink around here?"

"Think that's really what you need?" Back behind the counter, Maggie flashed a sour look of concern. "Talk to her. Maybe by now she's calmed enough to listen to reason. You get all liquored up, I'll take your keys and you won't be able to even see her."

"I'll take my chances. Please, Maggie, just give me the whole damned bottle."

What his longtime friend didn't understand—would never understand—was that when Ellie chose her in-laws over him, she'd made quite a statement. She'd told him that no matter how much he'd hoped for a future between them, she didn't care anything about him. All along, he'd been nothing more than a substitute husband. Thank the good Lord he'd learned the truth before becoming the real thing.

ELLIE HADN'T HAD a worse Christmas ever, not even when she'd caught her mother strung out, turning a trick on their living room floor.

With Pia finally asleep, Ellie tidied to work off nervous energy. Helen had refused to hug her goodbye, but John promised to talk to his wife, and she did show just as much affection for Pia as ever.

Ellie bent to grab a wad of wrapping paper lodged under the sofa when her eye caught a glint of silver. She reached for it, only to find Deacon's cell phone. He'd silenced it that morning, not wanting anything to interrupt their special time. Ha.

Perching on the sofa, Ellie turned on the device, looking at the pictures. He'd taken so many. Videos, too. Pia's first spin on her bike. Opening her Cinderella Barbie and tin of pink M&M's with her name written on them.

Father and daughter favored each other. Ellie hadn't noticed before, but in the few shots she'd taken, it was clear they each had a cowlick on the right side of their head, and their smiles crinkled their eyes the same. Judging by her expression of pure bliss whenever Pia hugged Deacon, the little girl adored him. Ellie didn't have the heart to deny him seeing his daughter, but how awkward would shared custody be?

When he'd given Ellie her ring that morning, she'd been initially shocked. Then had felt guilty. Then... happy.

How could she now feel so sad? She'd fought for him with Helen, insisting Deacon was a changed man, but was he? The guy she thought she might one day marry would never have been so cruel. For all they'd done for her and Pia, Helen and John deserved more than the crash-and-burn SEAL method of bad news delivery. The navy might be great at getting bad guys, but when it came to any subject remotely related to sensitivity, it sucked.

DEACON DIDN'T NOTICE his cell phone was missing until the next morning, when he woke on his apartment's front porch. Maggie had called him a cab, but rather than face his friends, he'd chosen to bivouac.

Last he remembered seeing it, his phone had been on

the side table at Ellie's, right next to the Christmas tree. The tree he'd helped pick out and decorate. As much as he thought he'd wanted to start a new life with Ellie, he now wasn't sure he'd be comfortable being in the same room with her. He regretted pushing her toward marriage before she'd been ready, but he'd honestly thought their being together was for the best. Ditto for revealing the truth to Helen and John.

Cold, hungry and needing to pee, Deacon finally swallowed his pride enough to bang on the door.

"Where you been?" Garrett asked, still half-asleep. "Maggie called around 2:00 a.m. asking if you made it here all right. She has your keys."

"Yeah, I'm here."

"You might be here now," his friend said, "but where have you been?"

"I slept on the porch." Deacon headed for the hall bathroom.

"What porch?" Garrett followed. "All we have is a concrete slab."

Deacon washed his face and hands. "Damn sight better than a lot of places we've crashed."

"True."

He wandered into the kitchen. "We got anything to eat?"

Leaning against the nearest wall with his arms crossed, Garrett narrowed his eyes. "I'll make you an omelet, but why aren't you over at the promised land, otherwise known as a clean house with a willing woman and Christmas leftovers in the fridge?"

Deacon opted for bologna on white bread with mustard, then said, "I told Tom's folks everything, they freaked, Ellie freaked. Luckily, it was a nice day and

Pia missed the whole ugly scene by playing outside. Then Ellie handed me my engagement ring and asked me to leave."

"Holy family nightmare, Batman. You've had one helluva holiday."

"Tell me about it."

"Hate to make things worse, but just got word we're shipping out in twenty-four. If you've got anything you wanna say to your daughter or former fiancée, now would be a great time."

"I DON'T WANT TO SEE YOU," Ellie said at her front door. At least Deacon had had the manners to ring the bell instead of using his key, which she probably should get back. "Since you're here, take this."

She handed him his cell phone, which she'd set on the entry hall table.

"Thanks."

"Daddy!" Pia zoomed around the corner from the living room. "I missed you! Nana got tea!"

"Really?" He knelt, giving his daughter a hug. To Ellie, he asked, "Translation?"

"Helen and John gave her a beautiful silver tea set. It once belonged to Helen's mom, and grandmother when they were little girls. She was quite upset when she left."

Go ahead. Rub it in deeper. "I said I was sorry."

"Great. So am I." *Sorry we ever met.* "Why are you here?"

"Don't worry, me being here has nothing to do with you. I'm shipping out and got the luxury of advance notice. I wanted to spend a few hours with Pia—if that's all right with you?"

No. But how could Ellie deny him when Pia was so happy for his visit?

"Santa gave house, too!"

He again looked to Ellie, who stood with arms folded. "Helen and John also gave her a dollhouse—another family heirloom I pray she doesn't draw on with the magic markers you gave her."

"Whoa." Deacon scratched his head. "I've devoted the last few months entirely to you and Pia, and this snark routine is the thanks I get?"

She managed a strangled laugh. "Really? This coming from the man who knew how much it meant for me to tell Tom's parents about Pia myself? In my own good time?" Looking away, she said, "Go ahead, take Pia out, but bring her back by four. We're having dinner with Helen and John."

"So let me get this straight. All's forgiven with them, but I'm still in the doghouse?"

She opened the hall closet for Pia's hat and coat. "It's hardly that simple and you know it."

"Daddy, jump?"

He laughed, and even as the sound had once made Ellie's spirits soar, it now destroyed her.

"Peanut—" he kissed Pia's nose "—Daddy's not really up for jumping right now, but let's go find pizza. That always makes me jump."

Ellie dressed her daughter for the chillier weather.

"Ready?" Deacon asked their squirming girl.

"Yes, yes, yes! Pizza!"

Ellie opened the door, bracing herself against it. "Don't forget to have her home by four."

"Will do." He gave her a cocky salute.

"Deacon?" Mouth dry, heart pounding, Ellie wasn't sure how she'd even said his name.

"Yeah?" He was so handsome, it hurt. But beyond that, he'd betrayed her. She'd trusted him with her secret and he'd not only spilled it, but in a devastating way.

"Be careful on your deployment."

"Why would you care if I get hurt?"

"Mommy love you!" Pia hugged his leg. "Pizza! Pia love pizza!"

Sobs caught in Ellie's throat. *Damn you, Deacon.*

For a short while, their life together had been amazingly complete. Why had he gone and ruined it?

"For the record," he called out, "you're wrong in choosing to please Tom's parents the rest of your life over yourself."

"Nana!" That night, Pia lunged at Helen the second she opened her beach home's front door. "Daddy had pizza!"

Ellie's stomach sank. She'd hoped to keep Deacon off the conversational table, but try conveying that to a two-year-old.

"Hello, Ellie." John took her elbow. "Get in here, it's cold."

"Papa, I *tea'd.*"

"Really?" He raised his eyebrows while closing the door.

Ellie clarified. "That's her way of bragging we shared tea this morning with her formal silver. I even found a crumpet recipe. We had fun."

Helen burst into tears, tugging Pia into a hug. "I love you, baby girl. God help me, but I can't stop loving you."

"You don't have to," John said. "We talked about

this. Our girls still need us. Ellie did nothing but try to protect us from a secret we might never have needed to know."

Helen looked to him and nodded.

"I'm sorry," Ellie said to Helen. Tears streaming down her cheeks, as well, she admitted, "You're the only true mother I've ever had. I can't lose you and Tom." *And Deacon? How do you feel about losing him?* Truthfully, horrible, but how did she even begin forgiving him for what he'd done?

Holding out her arms to Ellie, Helen said, "Next time you two make crumpets, mind if I help?"

"I'd love nothing more." With both women crying, sniffling messes, John and Pia joined in on their group hug.

Bored with crying, Pia said, "Nana ice cream?"

Helen laughed. "Yes, honey, you know your nana always has lots of ice cream."

DEACON AND HIS TEAM had hiked a good twenty miles inland from the Gulf of Aden. A group of allies were outgunned and needed help evening up a fight.

His night vision scope was giving him a headache, and again he found himself with too much time to think.

What'd happened?

How had he gone from his chest feeling swelled with happiness to now being tight with dread—not just about losing Ellie and a huge amount of time with Pia, but this mission. It'd felt voodoo from the start. They'd landed a few miles off course, encountered enemy fire where scouting reports had said there would be none, and now, two klicks from their destination, initial lead teams reported nothing where there should've been an encampment of at least a hundred men. SEALs were in the business of giving surprises, not being surprised. A fact that only increased his dread.

YOU WERE WRONG in choosing to please Tom's parents the rest of your life over yourself.

On her own at the boutique the Tuesday after Christmas, Ellie couldn't keep Deacon's words from messing with her head. Folding T-shirts, listening to Maroon 5 while outside a light snow fell and the scent of her favorite candy-cane candle filled the shop, she should've been content. Pia was having fun and hopefully learning a little at nursery school. They were both meeting Helen for a late lunch at their favorite teahouse. Life should've been good, so why did she feel empty?

As if she'd lost her best friend for a second time?

She liked to blame Deacon for what had happened on Christmas, but could she have been just as much to blame? She'd promised him that she'd reveal the whole truth to John and Helen by then, but had failed. Had she been wrong in sending Deacon away?

Pia constantly asked about him, which only weakened Ellie's resolve to cut him from their lives. Sure, now that he was deployed, it was easy enough to pretend he'd never been with them, but what would happen when he returned? When her daughter wanted him to play catch and throw rocks and tickle?

Cuddling with him had felt so good. So right. But that was before he'd betrayed her trust.

Did he? her conscience asked. *What about you betraying him?*

How many times had he begged her to let the whole world know he was Pia's dad, yet she'd denied him?

Over and over, he held back the news that, legally and morally, he had the right to share. Why? For her.

Staring out at the deepening snow, Ellie hugged herself. What had she done?

And why, when she most wanted to talk to Deacon, did he have to be a million miles away?

Finishing up the shirts, she tried consoling herself by assuming he'd be home soon. But then she remembered the dark day she'd learned Tom wouldn't be coming home, and worry that lightning could strike her life twice chilled her to her core.

Chapter Twelve

"Enemy fire! I repeat, high rate of enemy fire!" Deacon dodged left, then right. They'd been outfoxed once, but not again. With most of the team already having gained high ground, and thus tactical advantage, Deacon was almost there. Then he was hit.

Just in the calf, but it hurt like hell.

Ignoring the pain, he kept running, but then another bullet struck, this one a direct hit on his radio. Another pinged off his helmet, royally screwing his night vision.

Tearing off the useless goggles, he threw them aside and kept running.

When grenades exploded in front of him, cutting him off from his team, he changed course. It would be dicey making his own path, but at the moment, he didn't have another choice. He'd volunteered to stay behind, ensuring a trap they'd set would be tripped. It had, successfully eliminating at least ten enemy targets. But at what personal cost?

Running, running through darkness lessened only slightly by orange-red violence, he kept one thing in his mind—Pia. No matter what, Deacon had to stay alive, because when he got home, he intended to be the best dad ever. And to do that, he also realized he had to get over his issues with his own father.

As for Ellie, hindsight had brought remarkable clarity. He'd not only been a fool for believing the two of them had a chance, but he'd been a horrible friend. Tom—his memory—deserved more than Deacon moving in on his girls.

If he made it out of this hellhole in one piece, Deacon vowed to steer clear of his best friend's wife.

THREE WEEKS HAD PASSED since Deacon deployed, and Ellie was as cranky about his absence as their daughter was. Day by day, they went through their routines, but with Deacon not around, colors had faded. Flavors had dulled.

When the doorbell rang on a sunny Thursday, though Ellie was still plenty miffed with Deacon, part of her secretly hoped to find him at the door. Deacon still had his key, but as respectful as he was, until they'd worked out their issues, she appreciated him taking things slow.

She opened the door with a strange mix of emotions—fading anger and, yes, anticipation.

Pia came running. "Daddy! Daddy!"

"Mrs. Hilliard?" It was the base commander, William Duncan, and his aide.

Ellie's stomach tightened.

"No," she said with a vehement shake of her head, clutching Pia to her side.

"Ma'am, may we come in?"

"Daddy?" Pia peeked out at the men.

Five minutes worth of nerve-racking pleasantries later, Commander Duncan said, "Though I know you and Chief Petty Officer Murphy called off your recent engagement, we were surprised to find your little Pia is officially listed as his next of kin."

The man's voice droned on and on, but all Ellie heard was sick ringing in her ears. *No, no, no...*

"...and so you see, ma'am, while SEALs never willingly leave a man behind, and this search is ongoing, for practical matters, I have to inform you and your daughter that Deacon Murphy is missing and presumed—"

"Don't say it." Rising from the sofa, Ellie checked on Pia, whom she'd sent out to the deck to ride her bike.

"Ma'am, we wouldn't be doing our jobs if—"

"Do you even remember coming here for Tom's wake? Are your men so disposable to you, sir, that you can't recall it's been barely a year since you were last in my home? What? You weren't satisfied with taking just my husband? Now you had to go back for my fiancé?" Ellie didn't care that she was being hysterical.

"Ma'am, my sources told me you and Deacon were no longer engag—"

"Well, maybe we are," she all but shouted. "Maybe I now realize what a horrible mistake I made in ever letting him go."

Crying so hard she could barely breathe, she heard the commander's aide ask if there was someone he could call to help her through this difficult time. But she was too shaken to answer. This couldn't be happening again. Not with Deacon. Yes, she'd been furious with him, but never, ever would she have wished him dead.

Little good that realization did, now that he was gone....

"Is she going to be okay?" Ellie heard Helen whisper to John. She wasn't sure who had told them the news, but she needed them now more than ever. Only two days had passed, yet it might as well have been a week. Time had lost all meaning and she wasn't sure how to regain control.

"Don't know," John said.

Poor Pia didn't know what was happening. All she understood was that Mommy was sad.

"Honey," Helen said to Ellie, who lay on her side in bed, staring out the window. "It's such a nice day, John and I are taking Pia to the park. Want to come?"

"No, thank you." She'd cried so much she had no more tears.

"Okay…" After rubbing her shoulder, Helen left the room, calling from the door, "We'll be back soon. I have my cell if you need anything."

What Ellie needed was a third chance.

In finding love with Tom, she'd had one amazing life. With Deacon, a second, only she'd thrown it away. All along, he'd been right. Initially, Helen and John had been understandably upset by her news, but they'd adjusted, just as Deacon had told her they would. Why hadn't she listened?

Drifting into a dark, fitful sleep, where her dreams turned Technicolor and her body sighed into Deacon's strength, she cried again, welcoming him home to her arms.

"Ellie," he said through layers of her subconscious, "wake up. I'm really here. It's me."

She rolled onto her back, certain she was dreaming. Slowly waking, she blinked, then blinked again. "Deacon?"

"It's me. I'm here. Wake up. We should talk."

She didn't believe her eyes, but how could her sense

of smell also be wrong? He must've come straight from the base, for he carried with him what only a SEAL's wife would recognize. Scents of jet fuel, sweat and the sea. He went anywhere, did anything. Had he also managed to come home to her?

"Deacon?" Cupping her hands to his face, she felt his nose and forehead and cheeks, and finally those precious lips. "Is it really you?"

"What do you think?"

Quivering with shimmering relief, her heart singing, she couldn't stop crying, but this time for joy. "I'm sorry for putting you through what I did. I should've told Helen and John right away. I was a fool, Deacon. Can you ever forgive me?"

"Done," he said. His sober tone failed to match the magic of his being with her.

"I still can't believe it's really you." She hugged him, but he gently, yet firmly, pushed her away. "Deacon?" Her gaze searching his, she asked, "What's wrong?"

"Have you forgotten how we left things?"

"No, but—" She reached for him again, but he pushed her away.

"I'm here to set up a formal visitation schedule with Pia. I assume you want to keep this between us and not resort to getting lawyers involved?"

Where was this coming from? Had she alienated him to this degree? "Deacon, you know you can see Pia anytime you like. I'm sorry I flipped out at Christmas, but you have to agree it wasn't a stellar time for either of us."

"You know what?" He sighed. "I'm done with this whole paternity issue. I'm not sorry about what went down at Christmas. In fact, if I had to do it over, I wouldn't change a thing. Your reaction—you siding with Tom's folks—was the wake-up call I needed. My proposal was stupid. A pipe dream for the way I wished our lives with Pia to be. I should've known from your initial shock at seeing my ring that you didn't feel the same. If I had, I could have saved us a helluva lot of aggravation."

"That's not fair." A slow trembling began deep inside, one Ellie wasn't sure how to control. "Of course I was surprised you wanted to marry me. But then it made sense. I'm sorry if I hurt you, but Deacon, you hurt me. You just blurting out my secret like that—"

"Correction—*our* secret. Where's Pia?"

"In the park. She's been asking for you every day. She didn't understand why I couldn't stop crying. I've only just realized how much you mean to me. How could I explain to her that her mom's the biggest fool in the world for ever letting you go?"

"Stop." Far from him being moved by Ellie's confession, he clenched his jaw. "I had a lot of time to think while I was gone. Funny, but life is never clearer until you're facing death square in the face. I kept dwelling on Pia—and Tom. And how I never meant to betray him by falling for you all over again."

At the window, Deacon pushed back the curtain, staring at the sliver of Atlantic barely in view. "I'll always be here for Pia. But Ellie, whatever it was we shared, it's over."

"SHH…" AT THE BOUTIQUE two days later, Ada held Ellie through her latest batch of tears. While outside, falling snow made it tough to see across the street, inside they'd been sharing small talk, while keeping warm steaming the latest dress shipment. Ellie couldn't even pinpoint what it was her friend had said that set her off, but in what seemed to be an alarming habit, it didn't take much to upset her these days.

"Everything's going to be all right," Ada said. "I've been seeing this new guy, Marcus, a serious Manhattan business tycoon. Well, honey, he's got friends who make Bill Gates look like a poverty case. Once we fix you up, you'll—"

Ellie grabbed another dress and sniffled. "You really think this mess with Deacon will be better by me seeing another man?"

"Everything looks brighter with a new man," Ada assured her.

Her friend's rationalization was so ludicrous, Ellie couldn't help but laugh.

"See? Just talking about men is perking you right up. Marcus is flying his jet down this weekend to see family. Should I have him bring Craig or Bentley?"

"Neither." After hanging her latest garment on the appropriate rack, Ellie collapsed onto one of the white leather lounge chairs. "What I want is to rewind time and do everything over."

"Don't we all?" Ada kept steaming. "Trouble is, if we had that magic button, where would you stop? Before you even slept with Deacon? But if you did that, you wouldn't have Pia."

"If your plan was to make me feel better," Ellie said, "you're failing."

"DEACON. What a nice surprise," his mom said on the phone a week after his return from the dead. He'd called right away to let them know he was alive and well, but this call was different.

He was seated on the foot of his bed, alone in the apartment, and at four-thirty in the afternoon, falling snow left his bedroom nearly dark. "Sorry I don't get in touch more often."

"It's okay," she said. "How are you?"

"Good." He forced a breath. "I, um, have something to share. Something I hope you'll be excited about."

"Oh?" His old dog, Cheesy, barked in the background. How long had it been since he'd seen the little guy? He had to be ancient in dog years.

"I have a daughter. She's two. Her name's Pia, and once I get a couple days' leave and clear it with her mom, I'd like to bring her to meet you."

For the longest time, his mom didn't say a word. Then she murmured, "That'd be nice, son. Real nice."

SINCE HER SPLIT WITH Deacon, Ellie had spent more time at the alcoholic outreach center where she volunteered. This afternoon, since Deacon had Pia, Ellie sat in the communal meeting room of Friends Helping Friends, waiting for Pandora. Her heart had always gone out to the young woman, but Ellie struggled with the fact that had her own mom sought help when Ellie was young, her whole life might have turned out differently. School might not have been such a struggle, and learning to trust might never have been an issue.

The center had been set up in a renovated warehouse, and today, sunlight streamed through the enormous windows. All the main walls were brick, with divider walls painted a cheery yellow. Potted plants and trees thrived on even the coldest winter day. Live-in residents were charged with caring for them.

Pandora strolled in fifteen minutes late. Her normally straightened blond hair was held back in a messy ponytail and dark circles adorned her eyes. She reeked of booze and cigarettes, and the smell made Ellie's stomach turn. Though her training had taught her to remain calm, instinctively, she wanted to rail at the woman.

"Hey." The blonde stumbled into a chair.

"What happened?" Ellie asked, her hands clenched together on the table.

"You know…" She shrugged. "Met a guy, we started talking, he had some wine and one thing led to another and— Oh, forget it. I don't owe you an explanation." Pandora waved Ellie off and stalked toward the door. "Never did like this stupid place. Everyone's always preaching. Screw it. Nobody's ever gonna give me my little girl back anyway, and for people like me, nothing ever changes."

"Whoa." Lips pressed into a thin line, Ellie followed. "You were so close to getting custody of Julia. How could you give up everything you've accomplished for just one night of so-called fun?"

Pandora laughed. "Once that wine hit my system, chased by a little vodka, it was sooo easy. Peace out." After flipping her the bird, Pandora left the building.

Stunned, Ellie backed onto the nearest bench.

How could you give up everything you've accomplished for just one night? The question struck a chord with Ellie. Hadn't she essentially done the same with Deacon on the night of Pia's conception?

Yes, but the only thing she'd stood to lose was her dignity. Recognizing he was the kind of guy out for a good time, she'd welcomed their hasty goodbyes—or had she? Had her wish to be free of Deacon as soon as possible been more a case of her leaving him before he could do the same to her? Looking back, she recalled that as she'd gathered her belongings from his apartment, he'd announced that he was leaving to go to the gym. Like every man before him, he'd left first. Just like her mother. *Like Tom.*

Since Deacon's return from his latest mission, all mystery had been removed from their relationship. It was no longer a matter of *if* he would leave Ellie for the second time, since emotionally he already had. For Pia, he'd become a pillar of strength and support. For Ellie, a crumbling rock on which she could never quite find adequate footing. When it came to being a father, Deacon had become everything Ellie wanted for their little girl. He'd come so close to being the same for her, so where had things gone wrong?

Oh yeah, she thought with a faint, sarcastic smile. Her mistrust and downright fear that once they learned the truth, Helen and John would leave her, like everyone else. But they hadn't.

Could it be possible that Deacon might also be amenable to second chances? Did Ellie even truly want that?

Resting her elbows on her knees, she leaned forward, cradling her face in her hands. What a mess she'd made of everything. And in the end, was she all that different from her mom or Pandora? Only Ellie's drug of choice wasn't booze, but mistrust.

Chapter Thirteen

On Tuesday afternoon, meeting up with Ellie at the outreach center, Deacon fastened Pia into her safety seat and kissed her forehead before shutting the car's back door.

"If you have a sec," he said, not entirely sure how to proceed, "I have a question for you."

"Okay…" Something about Ellie looked off. Her eyes were red and her complexion sallow.

"With your permission, I'd like to take Pia to meet my folks."

"In Texas?" Her gloved hand over her mouth, she stared off at the setting sun. "I—I don't think that's a good idea."

"Why? She's my kid, too, Ellie. I'm trying to be civilized, but if you want things to get ugly, then—"

"Take me with you."

"To meet my folks?" He shook his head and sighed. "You know what went down between me and my dad. You know how hard this is going to be. Tossing you into the mix? Impossible." Turning his back, he headed for the Jeep.

"Deacon, wait!" Ellie chased after him. "I think it's great you're making an effort with your folks. But think about it. If I'm there, I can not only help you with Pia, but if things don't go the way you hope with your dad, I'll be there for that, too." She flashed a faint, almost hopeful smile. She looked so pretty with the setting sun casting a red glow to her dark hair. Before Christmas, he'd have been sorely tempted to pull her into his arms. Now? He knew falling for her all over again was akin to playing with fire. But had he ever completely *un*-fallen for her?

"Why are you doing this?"

"Honestly?" Head bowed, she scuffed the sole of her sneaker against the concrete curb. "I don't know."

"That's not a reason, Ellie. Last thing I want is to fight with you, especially in front of Pia." He shoved his hands in his coat pockets. His breath was starting to fog in the cold, and his throat felt achy, as if he was catching cold. Only since he'd felt fine before running into Ellie, he knew a simple virus wasn't the problem.

"All right!" Raising her chin, she met and held his gaze. "You need a reason? Right now, I'm not sure I can handle losing Pia, even for a few days. The fear of almost losing you was too much, and I'm not in a good place."

"Aw, Ell…" He had to laugh. "You didn't lose me, but threw me away. I'll be the first to admit we had a good thing going, but looking back, it was broken from the start. With Tom and his folks always between us, I couldn't compete. Hell, I now realize it was never even appropriate for me to try." Opening his car door, he added, "You want to tag along to Texas, be my guest, but if you're having second thoughts about you and me? Please don't."

LONG AFTER TUCKING PIA into her bed, Ellie nursed a steaming mug of tea at the kitchen table and stared at photos of happier times. When she came across an image of Deacon and Tom standing side by side at the backyard grill, she pressed a finger to her husband's chest. "Hon, I need help. You have to know I never meant to hurt you or your parents. Pia was the miracle by-product of a night that was a little scary—but in an unexpectedly good way. Deacon was too much for me. Too intense. He's not as slow and tender as you. But then I doubt the poor guy ever saw much tenderness to even know what it is. You're the one who taught me."

Flipping through the album, Ellie came to the last page, the last family gathering documented before his death. Tom stood with Deacon in the calm Atlantic surf, Pia held between them, equally supported. Was there any way Tom could've known he wasn't Pia's biological father? Was this shot, and others like it, his subtle way of telling her it was okay? Accidents happen and when they produce miracles like Pia, they're actually a good thing?

Ellie closed the book.

She wished she believed in signs, but she was far too practical to look for messages from beyond. What she believed in—had unsuccessfully tried teaching Pandora—was being proactive. If you didn't like a part of yourself or life, change it.

As it was only ten, she punched Deacon's number into the phone. Just hearing his husky hello soothed her more than the honeyed cup of chamomile did.

"Deacon, sorry to call so late, but I would like to go with you and Pia to Texas."

"You're sure?"

"Yes." Though he couldn't see her, she nodded. One thing she'd learned from all those memories in the photo album was that, like it or not, through Tom, through Pia, their lives were irrevocably intertwined.

"Free this weekend?"

"I can be."

After an unbearably long pause, he said, "I'll make all the arrangements and let you know final times."

"T-thanks." She hung up, only to glance at the album. She could've sworn she'd closed it, but it was open again to the photo of Deacon and Tom holding Pia.

NO MISSION HAD EVER BEEN tougher for Deacon than the one he was currently on. It was bad enough seeing his father for the first time in a decade, but sharing that momentous occasion with Ellie and Pia came close to being more than he could bear.

The beige living room of his folks' suburban ranch-style home resembled a shrine to Peter. Photos and memorabilia lined the walls, shelves and mantel.

"Look at you," his mother, Sally, crooned to Pia. "What a big girl you are. Pretty, too."

"Doggy pretty?" Pia held up the stuffed animal his mother had given her.

"Very pretty," she agreed.

While his mother and Pia became fast friends, Ellie sat in a recliner, a polite smile frozen in place. Deacon's dad had gone MIA. Sick of the whole "everything's normal" routine, Deacon finally asked, "Where is he, Mom? He had to know we were coming."

"Clint's in his workshop." She fingered one of Pia's dark curls. "Ellie, I—" Her voice cracked. "I can't remember the last time I've seen a more beautiful child.

This is...too overwhelming." When she dashed for the hall, slamming her bedroom door closed, Deacon sighed.

"Sorry," Ellie said. "Not sure what you'd hoped for from this visit, but I'm pretty certain this isn't it."

"Yeah..." He stood at the fireplace, arms crossed, staring at the oil painting of his brother hanging above the mantel. "I thought there was a chance my dad would be over this by now. You being so tight with Helen and John made me wonder. You know, if it could be that way with my parents?"

While Pia roamed the room, humming and exploring, Ellie silently came to him, slipping her arms around him for a hug. As much as he knew he should push her away, he wasn't strong enough. Even worse than being rejected by his father was knowing he could never have the special relationship he craved from the one person he'd come to need most. He might've become adept at physically avoiding Ellie, but that didn't mean he'd freed his mind of her.

"Find him," she urged. "Tell your dad exactly what you're feeling. Maybe he'll be receptive, maybe not, but at least you'll know you've done everything you can to attempt to repair what you once had."

"That's just it." He laughed and finally found the strength to give Ellie a gentle push. "There's never been a real foundation between us. I'm sure there were worse fathers out there, and my dad was always physically present, just not for me."

Ellie reached for him again, but then seemed to think better and shoved her hands in her jeans pockets. She looked so vibrant in a red sweater, like a candy apple decorated just for him. Only she'd never been *his*. She belonged to Tom. That's how it would always be. "We came all this way.... Talk to him, Deacon."

A nerve ticked in his jaw. "Will you and the munchkin be all right in here on your own?"

"Absolutely." Her smile bolstered him through and through. "We'll catch up on our reading." She nodded toward stacks of *Sports Illustrated*.

"Dad and Peter used to plan for when he'd one day be on the cover. I remember thinking I'd be happy for that day, too, because then I wouldn't have to hear another thing about it."

"Don't think for a second my Peter wouldn't have gone pro had you not killed him." Deacon's dad stood in the entry hall, facing the living room, wearing the scowl Deacon remembered all too well. Amazing how years of accomplishment vanish beneath the scrutiny of a father's condemning stare.

"Nice seeing you, too, *Dad*."

He grunted before slowly making his way toward what had always been his favorite recliner. Age hadn't been kind. He was only in his sixties, but from too much smoking and hours spent in the hot Texas sun working construction, he looked at least ten years older.

"Dad..." Deacon forced a breath. "Thought you'd want to meet your granddaughter." Taking her from Ellie, he held his little girl on his hip. "Pia, this is your grandpa Clint. Can you wave and say hi?"

"Hi! Me Pia and me *love* ice cream!"

"Cute." His dad barely even looked at the girl. "Ever get around to marrying her mother? Your mom told me you two aren't even shacking up."

It took every ounce of Deacon's strength not to pummel his father. They might be related by birth, but that was pretty much their only tie.

Ellie's eyes shone with unspilled tears, and in that moment, Deacon cared more for her than he ever had his old man.

"Ell?" He passed Pia to her. "How about you taking Pia outside. I have a few things to say, then we'll head back to the hotel."

She nodded.

With his daughter safely out of earshot, Deacon couldn't fathom where to start. "I'm not sure what I came here hoping for. Now that I'm a dad, I guess I was curious to hear firsthand what I ever did that makes you hate me. Because when it comes to Pia, there's honestly not a thing I can even imagine her doing that would make me love her less."

"You 'bout done?" Clint reached for his TV remote. "UCLA takes on the Ducks in twenty minutes."

Was the man made of stone?

Deacon had a tough time wrapping his head around his father's degree of hostility. How had Clint kept such a firm hold on this anger for so long?

"Son…" Deacon's mom entered the room. Her eyes were red-rimmed from crying and she held a tissue to her nose. "I should have told you this years ago, but—"

"Hush it, Sally," Clint commanded. "If you're about to open up the past, I told you I never want to speak of that matter again and I meant it. I did right by him and that's all that matters."

"Is it?" She dropped her hands on her hips, and her tone held a vibrancy Deacon had never heard before. "Is it really, Clint? His whole life you've treated him like dirt, and I'm sick and—"

"That's 'cause he is dirt. Spawned from an unholy union I've done my best to forgive. Bowie Glouster is a low-down, son-of-a-bitch cowboy who not only slept with my wife, but knocked her up."

Deacon backed onto the sofa. The room was spinning and his mother was crying. Nothing made sense.

"B-because I made a vow before God," his mother managed to say through her tears, "I've tried making this marriage work. You drove me to Bowie. Even after, I've all but abandoned my needs for decades to satisfy yours, but no more." She removed her wedding and engagement rings and set them on the hall table. "You wanna spend the rest of your life cooped up in this mausoleum when you have an amazing, accomplished son still alive and needing you, be my guest. As for me, I'm done."

"Suits me just fine." The man who for Deacon's entire life had posed as his father chuckled. "Ridding myself of a whore and a bastard murderer makes for the best damned day I've had in a while."

"Wanna say that to my face?" Fists clenched, Deacon challenged the old man to get out of his recliner. Clint wasn't dealing with a scared little boy anymore. "What happened to Peter was a horrible accident. You want to believe different, go ahead, but anyone who matters knows the truth, and that's good enough for me."

ELLIE PUSHED PIA in a tire swing hung from a live oak in Deacon's parents' front yard. The day was lovely. Sun warmed her shoulders, and with temperatures in the low seventies, the early February southern Texas afternoon felt like spring. Pia's laughter fit in well with the birdsong and occasional insect's hum. What didn't fit were the raised voices coming from inside the house. While Ellie couldn't make out specifics, it wasn't a stretch to guess Deacon's reunion wasn't brimming with the sweet forgiveness she'd hoped it would.

When the front door opened hard enough to bang against the outside wall, Deacon ushered his mom outside, leaving it gaping. Ellie hustled toward them. "Everything all right?"

He tossed her the rental car keys. "Do me a favor and get Pia back to the hotel."

"S-sure." With his mother sobbing and Deacon holding another set of keys, Ellie had no idea what was next for him on the day's agenda.

"Grandma Sally sad?" Pia asked from her swing.

"She is, sweetie." Ellie lifted her child into her arms, then stooped to fetch her purse from where she'd rested it beneath the tree.

"Grandma need ice cream?"

"Probably, but I think your daddy's going to get it for her." Having reached the car, Ellie made quick work of settling Pia into her safety seat.

"Daddy fun."

"Yes, he is, sweetheart." Instead of the jealousy Ellie might've once felt for Pia's obvious adoration of her dad, she'd come to realize just how lucky her little girl was to have a loving father in her life. Apparently, Deacon had gotten nowhere in his quest to get to know his own dad.

THREE HOURS LATER, Deacon's mother pulled into the hotel's portico. Having spent all that time with her and Bowie, his biological father, Deacon felt more emotionally messed up than ever.

"Sorry doesn't seem adequate," his mom said from

behind the wheel of her Buick. "I…" Heels of her hands pressed to her eyes, she shook her head. "Do you have to leave town so soon? If you stayed longer, Bowie could meet Pia."

Not sure he was ready for a big, happy family reunion, let alone dragging Pia and Ellie into his familial catastrophe, Deacon shrugged. "Another time. I'm due back on base."

She bowed her head. "I understand."

Do you? In one afternoon, his whole life had turned upside down. Moreover, the reason for every self-doubt he'd carried, for having been so unlovable his own father couldn't stand the sight of him, had now become crystal clear.

"Well…" He hugged her more from a sense of obligation than really wanting to. "Take care."

"I will." She flashed a smile through her tears. "For the first time in forever, I have the feeling everything's going to be fine."

"I'm happy for you, Mom." And he was. But that didn't mean diddly about how he was supposed to proceed with his own life. He said his final goodbyes and then headed inside. Through the lobby window overlooking an indoor pool floated sounds of splashing and children laughing.

A second look netted him a vision of Ellie perched on the pool's edge. She'd rolled her jeans up and had her feet planted on the stairs where Pia waded and splashed. The sight of them engaged in such a fun, everyday act of normalcy tightened his throat to the point he was sure he'd have trouble speaking. Despite that fact, he needed them. To talk to Ellie, hold Pia, reassure himself that despite the chaos raging in his belly, he was fundamentally okay.

"Hey," he said from behind Ellie, removing his Topsiders before rolling up his own jeans to join her.

"Daddy!" Pia marched in place and splashed. Her excitement at seeing him made his eyes sting and his throat ache. "We swim pool!"

"I see that, sweetie. Looks like fun."

Ellie met his gaze and put her hand on his knee. That morning, he'd have politely pushed her away. Now? He'd never needed her more.

Placing his hand over hers, he squeezed.

A few rowdy, school-aged boys were playing catch with a football at the pool's far end.

"Boys bad!" Pia announced, handing him the tiny doll she'd been playing with. The thing had nine lives, as he was pretty sure he'd seen Ellie take it from her before.

"Nah." After putting the doll in his pocket, he drew her close, kissing the top of her head. "They're just horsing around."

"Horsies go honk!"

Ellie laughed. "Geese honk. Horses neigh."

"Neigh! Neigh!"

While their daughter splashed, Ellie asked Deacon, "How are you?"

He grimaced.

"That good?" she teased.

"Oh—prepare to have your mind blown."

She returned her hand to his knee and he let her.

"Turns out we're not the only ones who kept a paternity secret."

Her eyes widened. "Seriously?"

168		*A SEAL's Secret Baby*

Nodding, he said, "Seems Mom got busy with an honest-to-God cowboy named Bowie. She used to clean his house. One thing led to another and she had me. For the sake of his own reputation, Clint agreed to raise me under the condition my mom never see Bowie again. He eventually married, spent his life working a ranch on the edge of town. I have two sisters living in Dallas and my stepmom died of breast cancer three years ago."

"Wow. I don't know what to say."

"Not much you could say. Is what it is, and it appears I was unwanted from the start." He hated coming across like a whiny kid, but dammit, that's how he felt. As if his biological father hadn't cared enough to fight for him, and the brute who'd raised him had been even worse.

"Hey, you," Ellie said to their daughter, hefting her from the water. "Nap time."

"No nap! No!" the little girl cried through a yawn.

"Come on…" With Pia on her hip, she held out her other hand to Deacon. "Once she's conked out, we'll talk."

Chapter Fourteen

"Now…" Ellie partially closed the connecting door between her and Deacon's adjoining rooms. "Out with it. I want to hear more about this new father of yours."

He sat at a small table beside the window, resting his feet on the king-size bed. "Already told you everything I know."

"Was he apologetic over not introducing himself to you sooner? Do you look like him? Did you feel any sort of natural affinity for him? I want everything." She sat cross-legged in the center of the bed's floral spread. "You know, the details."

"Well…" Rubbing his hand along his whisker-stubbled jaw, Deacon looked to the ceiling. "He did apologize, but considering my mom had begged him to keep the whole matter private, I suppose his hands were tied. We do look alike—would've had the same nose if mine hadn't been broken three times. As for liking him…" He lowered his feet to the floor, resting his elbows on his knees. "He was all right, I guess. The visit felt surreal. But the whole time I was there, I found myself wishing you and the peanut were with me." Pressing his hands to his face, Deacon admitted, "It was all a little much. I've been shot and it hurt less."

Ellie scooted to the edge of the bed. She wanted to take his hands, reassure him that to her and Pia he meant the world, but would he reject her? She wasn't sure her ego could bear it. On the flip side, at a time like this, when a friend truly needed her, should she be focusing on herself?

Going for it, she cupped her hands over his, melting from the sensation of even this light touch. She could deny it all she wanted, but whether it was wise or not, their chemistry was undeniable. Again, not even remotely appropriate thoughts, considering the topic of conversation.

"For what it's worth," she said quietly, her voice barely audible above the window air conditioner's hum, "I'm sorry. Guess if Tom were alive, we'd have eventually found ourselves in a similar rocky paternity situation with you."

Deacon groaned, but didn't pull away. "Don't remind me."

"What's next?" Her heart really did go out to him. "Planning another visit?"

"No." He stood, and in the process, broke their fragile bond. "Too much water under the bridge. It's all a mess."

"It doesn't have to be," she offered. Staring out the window at the overgrown lot behind the hotel, he looked so alone. She wanted to do something, say anything to help him out of his funk. But how could she do that when, in the time they'd known each other, she'd only added to his problems? "Give Bowie a chance."

"Honestly?" He turned to face her, blowing her away with the sadness in his eyes. "I just want to get the hell away from this place. Want to call the airline and see if they have an earlier flight?"

"YOU'VE GOT TO BE KIDDING!"

Finally off duty the Monday after his trip from hell, Deacon shared a driftwood log on the beach with Garrett, while waiting for Tristan to finish chatting up a hot redhead. He'd filled his friend in on the highlights, leaving out the part when Ellie had held his hands, and for the first time that weekend he'd felt as if everything would be okay.

"Your mom and this dude kept that huge a secret for that long?" Garrett shook his head. "And they say small-town gossip is a force to contend with. Sounds like your town's rumor mill is busted."

"True." Stretching his legs in front of him, Deacon slipped his hands into the front pouch of his gray hoodie. The ocean was restless, like him. He breathed in the salt air, allowing it to calm him like nothing else ever had—except Ellie. A notion that only riled him all over again.

"I'm almost afraid to ask, but how did things go with Ell? You two kiss and make up?"

Deacon shot his supposed friend a glare. "You know how I feel about her, man, but I just can't go there—especially considering my newfound rocky family history."

"Okay, whoa." Garrett held up his hands. "How is any of this worse than what you had going on with your original dad? And what does any of what's going on in Texas have to do with you and Ell starting a family with Pia?"

"Just does." Arms folded, staring out to sea, Deacon

seriously wished he'd driven to the base himself that day instead of riding with Tristan. "When I was lost on that mission, I couldn't get Tom off my mind. I kept seeing him in those last few seconds. The look in his eyes when he asked me to take care of Pia and Ell. He begged me to do right by them, but he never asked me to make them my own."

Garrett whistled. "That's heavy. But still…ever think Tom might've had a clue about Pia being yours?"

"No way."

"Think about it." Garrett paused a long time before speaking again. "If he had, then maybe what he really needed was for you to take over his job."

VALENTINE'S DAY FELL ON one of Deacon's usual Thursday-night outings with Pia, meaning the moment he was off duty, he would stock up on a mammoth teddy bear practically taller than her, and a chocolate heart.

His daughter was easy, but what should he do about Ellie? True, they'd gotten along better lately, but that didn't mean he was any closer to considering her *his* girl. Garrett's question on the beach still hung like a smoky cloud in his head, tainting his every thought. What if he was right, and Tom had meant for Deacon to watch over his girls in every conceivable way?

Deacon sighed.

He'd grab a simple box of chocolates for Ellie.

It wasn't a declaration. Merely a gift.

So why did the whole issue leave him on edge?

"Where you off to in such a hurry?" Garrett asked, running to catch up with him on the way to his car.

"Big day," Deacon said, already halfway across the lot. "Gotta grab sweet stuff for my girl."

His friend grinned. "Ellie?"

"Get your mind out of the gutter. Pia."

"Sure." Pulling out his keys, Garrett added, "Makes sense. But we hoped you'd come out with us tonight."

"I would, man, but me and Pia have big plans— Wacky Willie's. Now that I've got the hang of navigating the crowd and finding booster seats and only ordering cheese pizza for the squirt, I get a kick out of watching her hurl skeet balls. You wouldn't believe how freakin' strong my kid is."

Garrett shook his head and smiled.

"What?"

"Nothing. Have fun."

When his friend turned toward his car, Deacon yanked him back by his sweatshirt sleeve. "What was the smile about?"

"Guess I think it's funny how you're in so deep you don't even see you and Pia and Ell are already a family." Garrett shifted his weight from one leg to the other. "The guys are talking. You're suddenly driving Tom's car with a kid seat in the back—a guy famous for being able to pick up gorgeous women anytime, anywhere. They're assuming it's only a matter of time before you seal the deal, but you—" he snorted "—you're oblivious to the way she looks at you. I didn't get it at the time, but even at that one-year anniversary dinner Tom's folks hosted, you and Ell had a connection."

"Mind your own business much?"

Garrett shrugged. "Just calling it like I see it. Have fun." He waved on the way to his ride.

Only because the CO's wife had pulled into the lot did Deacon refrain from flipping his friend the bird.

After this latest round of unsolicited advice from

Garrett, Deacon was hardly in a festive mood. On a good day he hated shopping, but when he was itching to land a punch, crowded store aisles weren't a good place to be.

In the end, he grabbed that extra box of candy for Ellie and got on with his night. Before learning he was a dad, it would never have occurred to him to put so much effort into the holiday. Deacon loved women, but he'd never been in a relationship long enough for Valentine's Day to mean much. Come to think of it, aside from his mom, the months he'd spent with Pia and Ellie were the longest he'd been with any females. And no matter what his friends thought, he fully intended to respect Tom's memory by not taking things further with his best friend's wife.

The only problem was, the longer he was around Ellie, the tougher it became to not touch her, hold her, seek her out when he was blue.

Deacon pulled up to the library only to find the usually bustling lot empty, save for Ellie's Subaru station wagon. Pulling alongside it, he rolled down his window, letting in the bitter cold. "What's up?"

"Daddy!" Pia shrieked from her safety seat.

"Can you tell she's excited to see you?" When Ellie laughed, aiming her smile right at him, Deacon grew all the more confused. The chilly evening grew warm. The dread he'd felt at the store turned to anticipation for what the night might bring. Hell, his pulse raced just hearing her voice.

"I'm pretty psyched to see her." *And you.*

"Hope it's okay," Ellie said above Pia's humming, "but since my group was apparently canceled, I'm looking for something to do. Mind if I tag along?"

"Depends…" He cracked a daring smile. "How brave are you feeling?"

Wincing, she admitted, "Valentine's Day reminds me of Tom, so I'm up for anything except sitting home alone."

"Then you picked the right pair to hang with."

Parking so he could ride with Ellie and their daughter, Deacon willed his pulse to slow. He was just hanging out with his daughter and her mom, so why did his heart race as if he'd won the lottery?

As Deacon jogged around his car, cold burned his lungs.

He lifted the hatchback on her station wagon, tossing their gifts inside.

Entering Ellie's vehicle was like stepping into another world. A warm, comfortable place where he actually belonged. Coldplay floated through speakers and Pia *vroomed* her favorite plastic car across her safety seat tray. In that moment, the mellow vibe—the sheer, simple peace and warmth—touched off a feeling of harmony in him he wasn't sure he deserved.

For the first time in a long time, he felt happy. But instead of reveling in the moment, Deacon was a little frightened by just how easy it would be to slip into this role.

"Okay?" Ellie asked, looking his way.

"Yeah." So why was his throat tight?

She stared an uncomfortably long time. "Where we headed?"

Though all day he'd planned to take Pia to Wacky Willie's, noise and human chaos were the last things he craved. "Take a right on Pinshaw, then follow it down to the beach."

"Are you crazy?" She shot him a sideways glare. "This afternoon's front has it feeling like eighteen degrees, with a wind chill of forty below."

"Give me a few minutes' prep time at the abandoned ice cream place and I promise, we'll have a great night."

TRUE TO HIS WORD, within twenty minutes after their arrival, Ellie sat on a log before a toasty campfire. Pia had curled up on the bear Deacon had given her, contentedly gnawing on a supersize chocolate heart for dinner.

"Daddy fun!" Pia declared between bites.

"Yes, he is." The building was made of cinder block, with most windows long since blown out by Hurricane Floyd. Even so, the walls sheltered them from the biting wind, and the dancing firelight wasn't spooky, but fun. Sweet wood smoke transported her in time to dozens of happy nights spent on this very beach. "Not that I want your head to get one ounce bigger, but you SEALs truly are amazing. It would've taken me a week to pull this together, and even then, I'd have needed lighter fluid and a grenade to start the fire."

His handsome face sported a half smile as he stared into the flames. "So what you're essentially telling me is that if I'm planning a trip to Antarctica, you should not be first picked on my team?"

"When you put it that way," she teased, "you make me sad. Like I'd also be last picked for your dodgeball team."

He laughed. "A true tragedy, considering how often I play." Though he occupied the log alongside hers, she resisted the odd craving to tug him closer. On a night like this, cuddling was in order. It was Valentine's Day, after all.

But Deacon wasn't her Valentine.

"How have you been?" she asked. "Since Texas, I feel like I've seen you lots in passing, but we haven't had a real chance to talk."

"I'm all right."

His dropped gaze told her he might not be telling the whole truth. It would be understandable if he preferred keeping his demons close, but she would've liked to help. For her, believing she'd lost him had been a game changer. She'd realized how inconsequential her worries over exposing her secret had been in comparison to Pia—and her—losing this amazing man who'd become part of their lives.

But even though she knew Deacon to be a wonderful father to Pia, Ellie found herself constantly wondering what he meant to her. On the physical side, her heart raced whenever he was near, and his lightest touch turned her insides to jelly.

"Mom's called a few times. She and Bowie are planning a visit."

"That's good." Ellie leaned forward, wishing they were emotionally bonded enough for her to give him a hug.

"Is it? I told them maybe another time." Staring into the fire, he said, "Lately, I've been thinking I'd have been better off never even going to Texas. I had this pipe dream that somehow introducing Pia to my parents would make everything all right, but instead, it ripped our whole family apart."

"But, Deacon, seriously? You've told me even as a kid you recognized your home life was hardly idyllic. Might not seem like it now, but in the long run, this could change everything."

Meeting her gaze in a painfully direct manner, he asked, "Mind if we start that change by switching the subject?"

"Sure." She forced a smile. "How was your day?"

He laughed. "Nice and ordinary." Reaching into his jacket pocket, he withdrew an adorable miniature box of chocolates. It could only have held four, but they never ended up tasting as good as receiving them felt. "I almost forgot I grabbed a gift for you, too."

"Thank you." It was silly how her eyes welled. "I've been pretty bummed all day, so this means a lot."

"I wasn't sure if a gift would even be appropriate." He met her gaze, then quickly looked back to the fire. "Last thing I want is for you to get the wrong idea."

Like he might actually enjoy her company?

"Not that I'm saying you're not worth a little candy, but...oh hell, I butchered this big-time."

"Hell!" Pia blurted.

"Bad word," Ellie corrected. "Daddy didn't mean to say it, right?" A nudge in his direction prompted a nod.

"Sorry, peanut. Sometimes Daddy says grown-up words he forgets you're not ready to hear. I'm very bad."

"Time out?" she suggested, her chubby cheeks coated in chocolate.

"Probably," he admitted with an exaggerated nod. "How much time should I get?"

"Twenty-one hundred million!" Her laughter dissolved the tense atmosphere.

"That long?" Deacon whistled. "That's an awful lot of time. Is there something else I could do for punishment that wouldn't take my whole life?"

"Kiss Mommy! Say sorry!" Pia's suggestion had her excited enough to clap.

Ellie cleared her throat and said, "I think Daddy learned his lesson. He won't use a bad word again."

"Kiss Mommy! Kiss Mommy!"

"All right, peanut." Deacon finally relented when Pia's chanting got out of control.

Ellie's heart raced. He wasn't really going to kiss her, was he?

While he inched closer and closer, she felt the oddest panic. She couldn't breathe and her mouth felt as if it were filled with sand.

"Sorry," he said, barely loud enough for her to hear above their daughter and the crashing surf and, loudest of all, her heart pounding in her ears. "I promise not to say any more bad words."

He aimed for Ellie's cheek, but then the fire popped, sending him off course and directly against her mouth. For the briefest of moments, their lips touched, igniting a spark she'd prayed had been long since been put out.

Hanging back, his breath warm against her face, Deacon said, "Damn…"

"Bad word!" Pia clapped. "Kiss Mommy! Say sorry!"

Ellie cleared her throat. "We, um, should probably leave."

Chapter Fifteen

I kissed Ellie.

If he lived to be a hundred, Deacon would never understand his lack of judgment in kissing her. He'd been trained to have split-second reflexes, so why hadn't he simply avoided her lips? Moreover, why had he succumbed to the taunting of a two-year-old? Landing his mouth square against Ellie's had been an accident, one he felt terrible about. Not because the kiss had been bad, but rather oh-so-good.

Before he'd even had a chance to take off his boots and grab a beer, the door opened and in sloshed his roomies.

"You're home early," he said to Garrett and Tristan. "And you stink."

Garrett laughed. "Cabbie said the same thing."

"Lucky for us the girls don't care." Tristan shoved his coat behind the nearest recliner. "Make yourself scarce, bro. Two plus two plus you make five, if you get my drift."

"Yeah, not so much." But reading between the lines, Deacon assumed ladies were soon to arrive.

Garrett held a pack of Oreos and had just swallowed

a stack of three. "You shoulda' been there, bro. Action hotter than that time we used napalm to—"

A knock sounded on the door, followed by muted giggles.

"Save that story," Tristan said on his way to greet their guests. "Love that freakin' story. Ladies…" With a Vanna White flourish, he gestured the women in.

Deacon groaned.

A few months earlier, he'd have been smack in the middle of this action, but the party scene was no longer for him. He'd gotten more excitement out of watching Pia make a mess of her chocolate heart than he ever had hitting bars.

He made a few perfunctory greetings, then took a couple beers from the fridge before escaping to his room. The sound level wasn't much quieter, but at least he had the privacy needed to try making sense of the night. Of why he still tasted Ellie's favorite peppermint lip balm. Of how he was even alive when his pulse had taken flight. Of how more than he wanted sleep or beer or silence, he craved one more forbidden kiss.

All of which pretty much made him the biggest jackhole on the planet. Ellie might've been his a long time ago, but he'd given her to Tom, and with Tom she would stay.

But only till death do them part…

However tragic it might be, Tom was out of the picture, making her technically fair game.

Deacon had cut back on his drinking the past few months, but that thought led him straight to his old friend Patrón.

"YOU'RE THE LAST PERSON I should be sharing this with," Ellie said to Pia while running a washcloth over her in the warm, sudsy water. "But how awkward was that kiss? Couldn't you have just died when Daddy's lips touched Mommy's?"

"Duck!" Trapped in her bath seat, Pia pointed to her favorite purple bath toy.

Ellie handed it to her. "The whole mess is your fault and you don't even care. In fact, seems like you laughed your way through pretty much every second of this disaster of a night."

"Quack, quack! Ducky kiss you!"

"Thank you, sweetie." Lucky for Ellie's heart, kissing a bath toy had zero effect on her pulse. "But seriously, you pull a stunt like telling Daddy to kiss me again and I'm grounding you from all your stuffed animals for a week."

Pia giggle-snorted. "Ducky funny!"

Ellie finally got her daughter clean and dry and snuggled into her crib. Unfortunately, she'd accomplished all of that by nine, which meant she had an awful lot of Valentine's Day left to fill.

Had she not flipped over an accidental kiss that was really no big deal, she might still be with Deacon, sharing stories in front of his fire. Instead, she'd had to act like a spooked teen. It had just been a kiss. So why could she swear her lips still tingled?

"I CAN'T THANK YOU ENOUGH for watching Pia on such short notice." Two weeks after the infamous Valentine's Day kiss they had so far successfully avoided discussing, Ellie stood next to Deacon outside of Friends Helping Friends. The weather was once again pleasant, and while Ellie had furthered her volunteer training, Deacon had played with Pia at nearby Foster Park. He held her on his shoulders now, jiggling her sneakered feet.

"My pleasure."

"How about I return the favor by fixing us some supper?" Trying to be cool, Ellie tied Pia's left sneaker, pretending it didn't matter how he answered. Her proximity to Deacon put her body on full alert. Being close enough to catch the clean scent of his aftershave tightened her stomach.

"Thanks," he said. "But it's been a long day and I have a half-dozen tech specs to read through." He waved a hand toward his car. "I should get going."

Was he oblivious to the awkward undertones between them, or did he just not care?

"Car ride! Car ride!" Pia kicked his collarbone.

Wincing, Deacon carried their daughter to Ellie's station wagon. "Sorry, sweetie, but Daddy has homework. Promise, though, we'll have a fun ride real soon."

Ellie had had enough. "We ever going to talk about it?"

"What?" Deacon developed a sudden fascination with Pia's safety seat.

"Don't make me get into specifics. I'm talking about what happened on Valentine's Day. Though it was an accident, I…" Where did she start? Not so long ago, she'd have sworn on her life that any attraction she'd felt for Deacon was long gone. But that one simple kiss had led her down a dangerous path she wanted nothing to do with, yet had been helpless to deny.

"Stop," he scolded, his gaze darting about as if he was checking to see if she'd been overheard. "This is hardly the time or place."

"Then when?" Head bowed, Ellie rubbed her eyes

with her thumb and forefingers. She couldn't remember the last time she'd been more frustrated. The man made her crazy.

"Leave it alone, Ell." Deacon had hoped that kiss was long behind them. *Like it is for you?* Was that why he replayed it in his mind a dozen times a day?

She snapped, "You're seriously pissing me off."

Faking shock, Deacon gasped, *"Language."*

"I so want to hit you."

I so want to kiss you.

Lord help him, but she was even sexier all fired up.

Ellie closed Pia's door. "Honestly, Deacon, I don't see why you have to make such a big deal out of this. It was a kiss. It wasn't planned, but just happened. And—"

He framed her dear face with his hands and kissed her again. Only this time, there was nothing accidental about it. He kissed her thoroughly and completely, and when he was done, he was incapable of anything but wanting her more. "Sorry," he murmured.

Touching her lips, she just stood there gaping.

"What? Want to dissect that one, too?"

"Beast." She slugged his shoulder, only to clasp her hand to her chest. "Ouch."

He took her wounded hand, kissing it better, all the while never breaking eye contact.

"You're horrible," she whispered.

"Never claimed to be anything else."

"He didn't?" The next morning at the boutique, Ada was the one folding double time. "And you liked that kiss, too, didn't you?"

Heat scorched Ellie's cheeks.

"Come on, just admit it. It's okay."

"But is it?" Counting out the cash drawer to open the register, Ellie said, "On the one hand, that kiss was divine. On the other, it was like tossing open Pandora's box—and we both know how much luck I've had with women named Pandora these days."

Ada rolled her eyes. "That girl was trouble from day one. Don't let her problems shadow you."

"Easy for you to say." Pushing the register's drawer shut, Ellie turned introspective. "Looking back on it, when Deacon proposed at Christmas, I should've stuck by him—for Pia's sake."

"Ell, it's all right for you to enjoy your life. Not gonna lie, Deacon's a fine-looking man. I can't even imagine how good kissing him and more must be. So why are you denying the inevitable?"

"How is anything between us a foregone conclusion?" Outside, a cold rain fell. It seemed lately that the weather was as fickle as whatever she and Deacon shared.

"Easy." Having finished tidying T-shirts, Ada moved on to shoe racks. "Because you've got the hots for him, and no matter what he says, I'm pretty sure he has them for you, too."

"And? What does it matter? He's stuck on believing his being with me is betraying Tom's memory. And what if it is? What if right now Tom is looking down on me? Shaking his head in shame?"

"Girl, please…" Ada marched to the front door, inserting her key in the lock. "I said it before and I'll say it again, you are a full-fledged mess. For Pia's sake—for your own—put us all out of our misery and ask that SEAL to marry you."

LONG AFTER PUTTING PIA to bed that night, Ellie struggled to figure out where she and Deacon stood. What was wrong with her? How had one accidental touch of his lips to hers launched such a craving for more?

Not that she was a psychiatrist, but she guessed her attraction for Deacon stemmed not only from the memory of their one shared night, but to his having been Tom's friend. She was only looking to the familiar to fill the emptiness Tom's absence created, right?

Wrong. That discounted the fact that the more she was around Deacon, the more she truly enjoyed his company. Whether tossing rocks in a quarry or sharing a bonfire, they always had a good time. He was great for Pia, and as much as Ellie hated to admit it, he'd been right to expose her secret to Helen and John. Maybe he hadn't done it by her preferred method, but like ripping off a bandage, the pain had been short-lived.

She tried calling him, but got voice mail.

An hour later, she tried again.

Two days after that, Ellie lost count of how many times she'd tried getting in touch with Deacon. Pia had asked about him so much that now Ellie was worried. He had to have been called out on a mission. It wasn't like him to disappoint their daughter.

Standing at the kitchen sink, mindlessly scrubbing Pia's plastic cow-patterned cereal bowl, Ellie refused giving in to tears or fear. When Deacon safely returned—and he would—things between them had to change. Once and for all, she had to know where they stood.

DEACON HAD LAIN submerged in six inches of brackish water, covered in reeds, his gaze never leaving his

M82A1 sniper rifle's sight, for twenty-six hours. Until the target left his suspected hideout, here Deacon would stay—no matter how long it took. Garrett was on his left, Tristan on his right. With no clue as to when they might be called on by their superior officer to deliver a trio of kill shots, talk was on an as-needed basis. Meaning Deacon had had far too much time on his hands for mulling over problems back home.

He'd wanted to let Ellie know he was leaving town, but this mission had come about too fast.

Once again, he found himself in the unwanted position of dwelling in the past. Wondering what Tom would want in regard to his little family.

Ever occur to you Tom was your family?

True. The day he'd met Tom in BUD/S had been the day Deacon abandoned the screwup persona he'd been cultivating in Texas, to dare hope for something more. In the SEALs, he'd found honor and excitement and an odd sense of stability in spite of scheduling chaos. Lately, with Ellie and Pia, he'd found the two of them only enhancing his already full life. What had happened on their recent trip already seemed a million miles away.

As for that kiss?

Considering how often the memory came to his mind, might as well have happened ten minutes ago.

EASTER CAME AND WENT.

Fourth of July.

Ellie had lost count of the number of times she'd tried calling or emailing Deacon. Through the wives of men on his team, she'd learned what she'd already deduced.

He was on an extended deployment in an unknown location for an unknown period of time. Blah, blah, blah.

At Helen's annual Labor Day picnic at their beach home, Ellie hung back from the crowd, nursing a watermelon martini in the shade of a big umbrella.

Almost three, Pia ran wild on the beach, never more than a few feet from her doting grandmother.

Staring out at sea, Ellie wondered of Deacon, *Do you spend as much time thinking about me as I do you?*

DEACON'S TEAM HAD BEEN in transit for the last three days. Three days during which he'd found himself afraid of getting home. As much as he wanted to see Pia, he wasn't sure where things stood with Ellie.

Back on base, he sat through a day's debriefing and then was finally free. He rode his Harley along the shore until dark, loving the speed, the freedom, the briny scent of sea not laced with gunfire sulfur or the coppery tinge of blood on his tongue.

Pia's third birthday was only a week away and he wanted to be back in her life, but first he had to get himself mentally together. The mission had been a bitch. They'd lost a man and sometime in the next week there would be a funeral.

Coming on the heels of the anniversary of Tom's death, it was all a little much. More than anything, he wanted to talk it over with Ellie. Even worse, he wanted her to hold him. Tell him everything was going to be okay. But he couldn't do that, could he?

At his apartment, he showered, and finally plugged in the charger on his phone. There were thirty-eight messages. Five from his mom. The rest from Ellie. Begging him to call.

As much as Deacon wanted to hear her voice, he turned out the lights in his room, crashed on his comfortable bed and fell asleep to the sounds of Garrett and Tristan playing with virtual guns instead of the real deal.

"I, AH..." Ellie shifted the still-warm Pyrex lasagna pan from one hand to the other. Garrett filled the apartment's open door. "Heard through the grapevine you guys were back. Thought you might be hungry." Nodding toward her car, she added, "I've got salad and garlic bread, too. Been a while since I've hung out with grown-ups, so Helen's got Pia for the night."

"Thanks for this..." Garrett took the pan from her, setting it on the entry table. "But you know he doesn't want to see you."

Her throat instantly tight, her mouth dry, Ellie nodded. "I figured as much, but Deacon can't avoid me forever, you know? I don't even know why he's acting this way."

Garrett shrugged. "Beats me."

"You honestly don't have a clue what's going through his head?"

"Sorry." He wouldn't meet her gaze. "All I know is my boy Deacon's hurting. Don't take this wrong, but I'm pretty sure you're the cause. He wants you and it's eating him up inside."

"W-wow." Garrett's statement hurt. "I'm just going to grab the rest of the food and then—"

"Stay..." Deacon emerged from the hall.

"Really," Garrett assured him, "I've got this."

"Thanks," Deacon said in an exhausted tone, "but it's past time for me to man up."

"Whatever." Garrett took the lasagna to the kitchen, grabbed a fork, then headed for his room, shouting over his shoulder, "Thanks for the grub."

"You look good," Ellie said to Deacon, not even sure why. He did. Oh, how he did. Big and tall, his skin ruddy from too much sun. His hair had grown out, as had his stubble, and the tank tee he wore showcased his muscles to an alarming degree. Last thing she wanted was to admit her attraction to him. It was proving hard enough for them to be friends. They would never be capable of sustaining more.

"Thanks." Glancing around her to the car, he asked, "Where's the munchkin? I've been meaning to get over to see her, but…"

"Listen…" A breeze caught Ellie's hair, curtaining her face.

On autopilot, he swept it from her cheeks, tucking it behind her ears.

"I'm sorry, Deacon. So sorry for whatever I did."

"You didn't do a thing. I've been a stubborn fool, trying to make sense out of what's happening between us, when there's no way—no need—to label it." He pulled her into a hug that felt more as if he was holding on for dear life.

And then he was crying. Not like she did, loudly and not caring who heard, but in heartbreaking choked sobs, into the crook of her neck. The SEAL community was tight-knit, and she knew they'd lost another man. It happened. All involved were adults and it wasn't as if the players didn't know war was a dangerous game. Two years ago it'd been her husband who'd died.

Now, another woman's husband.

Not that Ellie wasn't patriotic, but after a while it all

seemed senseless. Mandy and Neil had three little boys. No matter how many times Tom had tried to explain, Ellie hadn't understood why being a SEAL had been worth more to him—to all the men on their team and others—than their wives or children.

"Hell," Deacon finally said, wiping his nose with his forearm and his eyes with the heels of his hands. "I wasn't even with Neil when he went down. But it brought it all back, you know? Tom. Finding out about Pia. Everything. And…"

"I know." Now she was holding on to him. In this crazy world where it seemed everyone they cared for could be gone at any second, at this moment they had each other, and that's all that mattered. All of their other issues faded away.

Chapter Sixteen

"Look at Daddy, peanut!" Deacon made a goofy face for Pia, trying to lure a grin out of her for the camera. Ellie had planned a birthday party with cake and a Hello Kitty piñata, but the poor kid had come down with flu and spent her big day in bed. Just as well. The steady downpour would've made for a miserable houseful of sugar-hyped kids. Was it wrong that aside from Pia being sick, he was glad for the way things had turned out? He needed this day alone with the two of them. He'd been gone for so long, he craved time to catch up. "Look what I found for you."

The frog he'd brought her was not only age appropriate, but he had an art kit tied to the big guy's neck that she'd also be able to safely use.

"Thank you, Daddy."

"You're welcome, sweetie." Perched on the edge of her bed, he set the frog on the floor, comforting her by smoothing the hair from her fevered brow. "Want more to drink?"

She shook her head.

Seeing her sick like this would have hurt him anytime, but it was especially sad on a day she was supposed to be having fun. "I promise, as soon as you feel better, we'll do something amazing."

His little girl nodded while drifting off to sleep.

"She missed you." Ellie stepped up behind him, close enough for him to feel her heat. He'd hoped being apart from her would've squelched this attraction. He'd been wrong. *What about you? Did you miss me?*

"I missed her, too." He rose from the bed as gently as possible as to not wake her. In the kitchen, palms braced on the counter, he said, "We spent days in a village that had a lot of kids. Every time I saw one of them struggling for their next meal, it hurt. And I thanked God Pia was safe with you."

Transferring Pia's favorite oatmeal cookies from a platter to plastic bags, Ellie said, "I wish you had called."

"Sorry. We were in deep cover in the middle of nowhere. Some days I was afraid it would never end."

Outside, lightning cracked.

Thunder rumbled, loud enough to shake the small house.

Deacon wrapped his arms around her, holding her tight.

"Where is this going?"

"Wish I knew."

He asked, "Where do you want it to go?"

The look on Ellie's face said more than words ever could. "Deacon, I want us to explore what you started on Christmas. I face the same guilt you do when it comes to Tom's memory, but when you were gone, I realized that particular pain is nothing compared to the hurt of missing you when you're away."

"I want that, too, but I'm not capable of being the

man you need me to be—not yet." He kissed her deeply and surely, holding her in a way he hoped told her he planned on never letting go. While he wasn't sure he was capable of a permanent commitment yet, he had to convey that he wasn't just messing around.

All his adult life Deacon had been running from commitment, from the family life he thought would never be for him. But here he was, over the moon in-fatuated with a toddler and halfway there for her mom. Why couldn't he get it to stick in his thick head that he was also her dead husband's best friend? What was it about her that made him forget he had no business be-coming the head of a family, when he had no clue what an ideal family was even supposed to be?

"I'm not asking you for— Who am I kidding? Dea-con, I want to marry you. Pia adores you, and with time, I think the two of us could really click." Hands pressed to his chest, standing on her tiptoes, she kissed him. Seriously kissed him, until he wasn't sure his heart could stand it.

"SHE'S GOT YOUR LOVE for the water," Ellie mused to Deacon as they sat together on the isolated shore that Sunday, watching Pia frolic in the foamy surf. She'd removed her shoes and tights, and waded and skipped and laughed. "Tom's, too, for that matter. He loved tak-ing her here."

"I know." Deacon reached for Ellie's hand, but this time it was different. Instead of clasping their fingers together, he spread hers apart, easing his between them. The action struck her as shamefully intimate, yet im-possible to deny.

Resting her head on his shoulder, she sighed.

"Sure would make life easier if you told me what's going through that pretty head of yours, as opposed to me having to guess."

She laughed. "Would you believe me if I told you that when it comes to you, I have no idea what I'm doing?"

At that, he, too, had to chuckle. "Ditto. You make me nuts."

Nudging his shoulder, she said, "Nice we have that in common."

After sharing a simple, yet heartfelt kiss, he said, "The other night you talked about marriage. But what would you think if I moved in with you guys first? I want to wake up with Pia and help her get ready for her day. Read her stories and tuck her in at night."

"I want that, too." Ellie stared out to sea. "But now that I went and opened my big mouth about marriage, I'm scared."

"Of what?"

"I've grown to depend on you. So has Pia. But is what we share based on mutual love and respect for our daughter? How do I even know that what I feel for you is real and not some leftover of my feelings for Tom?"

Deacon frowned. "Ouch."

"Can you honestly say you disagree with anything I've just said?"

He took a piece of driftwood near his feet and stabbed it into the sand. "You think I'm not struggling with the same demons?" He stroked her hair. "Only I was there, Ell—with Tom at the end. He made me promise I'd look after you and his little girl. But to what extent would he have wanted me with you? It's bad enough I already staked my claim on his kid, but his wife, too?"

After exhaling sharply, he asked, "Do you have any idea what these constant questions are doing to me?"

Ellie laughed through her tears. "Yes, I do know, because I feel the same. But that doesn't get us any closer to figuring out what to do about it."

For the time it took the surf to caress the shore three times, Ellie gazed into Deacon's eyes. She wondered if he'd kiss her again. Craved him kissing her. Knew she shouldn't want him to, but was nonetheless obsessed.

"Ever wonder if it was me all along you were supposed to be with?" With the pad of his thumb, he stroked the sensitive skin of her palm.

She shook her head. "I don't want to go there. I *can't*."

"Just because you don't want to think about a fact doesn't mean it ceases to exist. I know you and I have something special, and lately, I've been thinking we owe it to ourselves to give the two of us a try."

His clenched jaw did little to make him any less attractive. If anything, this hardened determination that seemed to have settled over him only made her want him more. Tom had been a SEAL, every bit as physically strong as Deacon, but in a vastly more gentle way. Yet Deacon seemed to be changing, becoming less the bad boy she'd slept with so long ago.

"I don't know what to say."

She pushed herself to her feet, but he tugged her to his lap. "Just give me an answer. Am I in your life or not? I don't know when I'm shipping out again, and when I do, I sure as hell don't know if I'll be coming back. What time I do have, I want to spend with Pia." He kissed her. "And you."

"I'M HAPPY FOR YOU." Garrett pushed the last two boxes of Deacon's stuff into the back of Tom's old Jeep. "But are you sure this is what you want to do? You were all over the map when we got back. If this isn't what you want, one or both of you are going to end up hurt. Then what? Poor Pia's stuck in the middle of—"

"Who died and made you Dr. Phil?" Operating on less than an hour's sleep and a full day's training, Deacon was hardly in the mood for one of Garrett's philosophical lessons.

"Just saying…" Garrett held up the dead ivy plant some girl he'd dated had given Deacon. She'd told him he needed domesticating. "Want this?"

"What do you think?"

While Garrett deep-sixed the plant and Tristan called every woman on all three of their contact lists for the going-away party he was hosting, Deacon cleaned out his dresser drawers. All he had to move were his few personal effects. Clothes, a couple framed snapshots of his brother. Kind of ridiculous, really, that here he was over thirty and with nothing more to show for it.

Tristan came outside, swigging from a beer and downing a few of the boiled peanuts his mother regularly sent. "If you ask me, Woof here's jealous. I know I am. You're about to be living in the promised land, brother, getting your meals cooked and laundry done. Got your cute-as-a-button little girl." He whistled. "Better live it up tonight, my friend, because as of tomorrow, you're officially off the market."

"It's not like that—at least not yet." Deacon set his overflowing dirty clothes hamper by the Jeep.

"Uh-huh." Tristan laughed. "That's how you two made that pretty baby, right? Just being friends?"

Their buddy and fellow team member, Calder, knocked on the open door. "Room for one more at this party?"

"You know it." Tristan offered his can of peanuts. "Welcome. Once we get this dud out of here, we can return to our normally scheduled fun."

"Can't remember the last time I've been to a real grown-up party," Ellie shouted over the surging base of techno blaring through jumbo rented speakers. Unsure how to explain to Helen and John that she was attending an event celebrating Deacon's moving in with her, Ellie had hired a sitter for Pia. She'd asked Ada, but Ada had insisted on coming to the party, too.

"Yeah." Deacon led her out of the apartment and down to the pool. "Gotta say, my boys have outdone themselves with this one."

"How is it that every cop in the county isn't here?"

He pulled out a chair for her at one of the poolside tables. It was a warm, Indian-summer night without a breath of wind. "They invited all of them, plus the property manager and damn near everyone living in the complex."

"Ah…a shining example of SEAL ingenuity." Sipping her red wine, she tucked her loose hair behind her ears with her free hand.

"Why do I get the feeling you wouldn't appoint yourself head of the SEAL fan club?"

"Can you blame me?" She twined her fingers through the chair's plastic mesh seat. "My first encounter with a SEAL was you—and we all know how that turned out. I vowed never to speak to another of your kind, but then you introduced me to Tom and he showed me a whole new side of your tribe. He was sweet and gentle and loving and treated me—"

Leaning forward with dizzying speed, Deacon kissed her breathless. "You have any idea how sick I am of hearing your dead husband's praises? I loved the guy like a brother, but Ell, I'm not stupid. I know there's something simmering between us. Don't you want to explore that? If not for our own sake, then Pia's? We could be the total package."

She kissed him back. Deeper and slower, stroking his tongue with hers. He tasted of beer and pretzels and that bad-boy image she'd craved one long-ago night. And here she was now, wanting him all over again, without even fully understanding why.

"This is a bad idea…" He shifted her onto his lap, easing his fingers beneath the curtain of her hair.

"I know…" She slipped her hands under his T-shirt, loving the feel of his rock-solid bare chest.

Standing, kissing her all over again, he urged her legs around his waist, carrying her she didn't know and didn't care where.

He stumbled onto the grass and then up a short flight of stairs, eventually landing them on a pillowed bench.

"Where are we?"

"I think a gazebo."

Beyond caring, when he settled atop her, she continued with her exploration of his chest. He paused to remove his shirt, making her task easier. "Sure about this?"

She shook her head, but then nodded, slipping the thin cotton straps of her sundress off her shoulders. As much as she had reservations about being with him again, she couldn't deny that the only time she felt fully alive was when they were together.

With the party far away now, Ellie sat up while Deacon tugged at her dress. She wore no bra and when he leaned in to suckle her, the pleasure was intense enough to make her cry out.

"I'm not hurting you?"

"No." Tears stung her eyes. She'd lied. Yes, what they were about to share would be painful, but not in the way he thought. Why, she couldn't say. Maybe the angry words they'd exchanged on the beach, maybe the knowledge that with him living in her house, a reunion like this was inevitable... But she was tired of fighting reality. Tom might be dead, but she was alive. As much as he'd loved her, she had to believe he would never begrudge her the right to fully live.

"Hey..." With the pads of his thumbs, Deacon brushed tears streaming from the corners of her eyes. "If you're not ready, let's stop this now."

She shook her head.

Ellie wanted this man inside her. She needed to know that part of her was still operational. That she was still capable of giving and receiving pleasure.

Back to kissing, with his fingers between her legs, she blossomed from his touch. Moments—maybe hours—later she gasped when he entered her. It'd been a while for them both, and neither lasted long. What Ellie remembered most about their union was Deacon holding her afterward, brushing away more tears and then kissing her until she was incapable of wanting anything more than for him to enter her again.

Finally sated, with him clasping her close on the narrow bench, she used his biceps for a pillow, caressing the coarse hair on his forearm. "Thank you."

"Sorry."

His single word chilled her to her core. How could he be sorry about a beautiful event that'd been a year in the making?

"I've got to get out of here." In a move only a man with his strength could accomplish, he slipped out from behind her and stood, grabbing for the cargo shorts he'd worn commando.

"Why? Deacon, what's wrong?" She sat up and reached for her sundress, suddenly feeling shy.

"Everything. I thought the two of us being together would magically erase the guilt, but it only made it worse. And then there's my screwed up family." He pulled his T-shirt over his head. "What if that mess is genetic? What if my being around Pia only teaches her to be as dysfunctional and confused as me?"

Ellie stared at him in disbelief, fury rising within her. "Are you listening to yourself? Do you even remember our last time together? No? I'll give you a refresher. It went a lot like tonight—only a thousand times hotter. And then you left. I can now see you for the scared little boy you are. You're no good at commitment, which is why you only have one-night stands." Leaning into him, her face inches from his, she said, "I've got news for you. You, me and Pia could've had it all, but you ruined it."

DEACON SPENT THE NIGHT on the beach, all alone save for a bottle of cheap tequila he'd taken from the party.

His head throbbed.

A cold front had moved through.

And more than anything, he knew Ellie had been right. He had ruined everything—again—and this time he wasn't sure there was anything left between them to repair.

Rolling onto his back, hand on his forehead, he tried to figure out where things had gone so horribly wrong. He genuinely cared for Ellie and loved his daughter. Why had the same old guilt consumed him? The same fears that he wasn't good enough?

With the wind chill dropping by the second and the Atlantic whipped into a fury, he figured he might as well face the music. Sharing Pia as they did, he and Ellie couldn't exactly never speak again.

Given the stiff breeze, Deacon found his helmet a good ten feet down the road from his bike. As it had been downright balmy the night before, all he wore was a T-shirt.

Now that it had started to drizzle, he'd had January night dives in the Baltic Sea more pleasant than the ten-mile drive to Ellie's.

His garage opener was in the Jeep, which was in the garage, so he parked his ride in the drive and used his key for the front door. "Hello?"

"Daddy!" Pia jumped up from in front of the TV, where *Cinderella* was blaring. "I missed you! Katie babysitted me and we made cheese."

"Wow…" He hefted her into a hug, loving the feel of her warm little body.

"You're cold!" She giggled when he nuzzled her neck.

"I sure am." He gave a goofy growl. "Good thing I've got you to warm me up."

Setting her on her feet proved to be a mistake, for

she took off running and shrieking through the house, much like a crazed poodle his mom had had when he'd been in grade school.

"Spend the night in a bar? Or with another woman eager for you to share her bed?" Ellie stood in the hall dressed in jeans and one of Tom's old sweatshirts. Arms folded, lips pressed into a frown, she glared at him. He knew he deserved her anger, but to suggest he'd been with someone else?

"I'm here to apologize, but after that, you owe me one, too."

"Then where were you?"

Needing coffee, he bypassed her in favor of the kitchen. "The beach."

"It's, like, forty degrees outside."

"And?" Taking a mug from the cabinet beside the stove, he filled it with the fragrant brew, thankful Ellie already had some made. He chugged it hot and black.

"Have I mentioned how much I hate your stupid SEAL macho crap?"

"More times than I care to count. But apparently, you don't hate SEALs enough to not marry or sleep with them." The second he said the words, Deacon knew he'd gone too far. But then so had she.

Pia had begun to sing along with the movie.

Deacon sliced his fingers through his close-cropped hair. "I'm so not cut out for this. If you want to take Pia out for a movie or something this afternoon, I'll haul my boxes back to the apartment."

Eyes shining, Ellie nodded. "Thank you."

"That's it then?"

Focused on their daughter rather than him, she said, "Guess so."

"Don't be like this," he begged. "I said I was sorry. From the start, you knew I wasn't cut out to be a family man."

Grabbing her own coffee mug, she laughed.

"I wasn't trying to be funny."

"Oh, I know. The thing is, you're so focused on what you believe you can't be, you've missed the bigger picture, which is the amazing father and husband you've already become."

Chapter Seventeen

"You gonna survive this?" Ada stepped up behind her at the boutique's counter, offering a box of tissues. Though Ellie took one now, she'd prided herself on holding it together when they'd had customers that afternoon.

"Not sure. I feel stupid. Like I'm mourning the loss of something I never even had."

"Honey, no…" Ada wrapped her in a hug. "You did everything you could to make you two work. He's damaged to a degree you can't fix."

"I know," Ellie said past a sniffle. "But knowing that, why does it still hurt so bad?"

"Because you invested not just your time in him, but your emotions—and your child. You wouldn't be human if you weren't upset."

"Where do I go from here? How do I even start picking up the pieces? It's hard enough on me, but Pia doesn't understand why Daddy doesn't live with her."

"Ever think it's not your place to tell her?" Sorting the mail, Ada said, "Deacon made this mess for your little girl. Let him clean it up."

"BUNS!" DEACON'S CO shouted across the shooting range, where they'd been trying out new weapons.

"That's five in a row you've missed by a good six inches!"

Deacon clenched his teeth at the CO's use of his stupid nickname. He couldn't help it if women liked his butt. The name had always annoyed him, but never more so than today, when he wanted to forget any women existed.

When his shooting hadn't improved after another five hundred rounds, his CO called him aside. "What's going on with you? Woof says family issues. Hate to hear it, but you know you can't bring that stuff to work with you."

"Yeah. Sorry." Deacon began disassembling his rifle to clean it. "Won't happen again."

"Damn straight, because you're taking leave until you figure it out. This has been going on for a week and I can't have you possibly heading out on a mission with your head not in the game."

"Yessir, but—"

His CO waved him off. "Don't wanna hear it. Come back when you're not going to get yourself or someone else killed."

To say Deacon was pissed by this latest development would be a massive understatement. Ellie had already cost him his sanity. Now, his job?

He'd moved his stuff a day earlier, so spent the rest of the gloomy afternoon unpacking and cleaning carpet stains from the party. Since Deacon took back his old room, Calder now bunked in the apartment's office on a futon. With him only twenty-three, his spine could take it better than Deacon's.

By the time Garrett got home, Deacon felt like a

caged housewife, and all but pounced on his friend the moment he'd removed his coat. "Don't lose that just yet. Wanna go to Tipsea's?"

He blanched. "After the fun you missed out on today, sorry man, but I've gotta grab some *z*'s."

"What about Tristan and Calder?" Deacon could go on his own, but the bar was way more fun with friends.

"Tristan mouthed off and pulled a bonus run. He and Calder are in the midst of a bromance, so the kid stuck around to keep him company."

"Great. So they're probably not gonna party, either?" Deacon fell into a recliner.

"Don't mean to get into your business, but what's wrong with you, man?" Garrett grabbed a beer from the fridge, then popped the top.

"Regarding what?" Deacon turned on the Xbox, tossing the spare controller at Garrett when he took the chair next to him.

"Come on, man, seriously?"

Sighing, Deacon paused the game he'd only just started. "If you're talking about Ellie, I'd prefer to avoid that topic."

"I'm sure you would," his friend said with a sarcastic laugh. "Trouble is, any fool could see being away from her and Pia is eating you alive. As long as I've known you, you've never willingly cleaned the bathroom, but now it's sparkly fresh. What gives?"

"Nothing. Leave it alone." Had Deacon needed counseling, he'd have called a professional.

"I would, but there are rumblings of another trip coming up and I selfishly want you with me. That can't happen until your head's in a better place."

"Oh—" Deacon snorted "—and I suppose you know where that is?"

"Don't be stupid. I saw how happy you and Ellie were the night of our party. I've seen your face light up with Pia. I also saw you and Ell getting busy and—"

"Aw, you watched." Deacon threw down his controller. "Not cool, man."

"Relax. Once I caught a peek of your bare ass, I turned away. What happened? You two seemed like you had it all figured out."

"I thought so, too, but then we—" he cleared his throat "—you know, and for me at least, everything changed."

"How so?" Garrett finished off his beer.

"I couldn't get past the guilt. Then there's my whole screwed up family. I don't want to bring that mess to Pia. She deserves better."

"Like having no dad at all?"

Turning introspective, Deacon admitted, "For me, it would've been the lesser of two evils. You grew up in the equivalent of a perfect sitcom family. You have no idea what it was like for me."

"Granted." Garrett headed to the kitchen for another beer. "But Pia got a do-over with you, and you've got one, too, with your new dad. Take this time off and go see him—*really* see him. Get to know him, and maybe you'll figure out something about yourself."

"Have a safe trip." There was so much more she wanted to say to Deacon, but as he lifted Pia into the station wagon outside the library, after their usual Thursday night together, Ellie's mouth was dry and her heart was aching. What was wrong with him? Why couldn't he see how perfect the three of them could be?

"I will." He handed her a folded slip of paper. "You have my cell, but here are a few other numbers, too. You know, in case something comes up with Pia."

"Nothing's going to happen that I can't handle." The night was pleasant enough, crickets chirping and the library buzzing with activity, so why did Ellie feel so empty and unfulfilled? Why had her grief support group, which she usually found uplifting, left her melancholy and confused? The truth was, since making love with Deacon she was no longer mourning the loss of Tom, but of him. Though Deacon was still there for their daughter, for Ellie he was gone.

"You don't know that. Just take it."

She did, cramming the paper into her purse. "When are you coming back?" She'd almost asked when he would be home, but did he even know what a home meant?

"Not sure."

"Okay, well…" She might've once given him a hug, but now she secured her purse higher on her shoulder, gripping the leather handles for dear life. If she hadn't, she might've been tempted to smooth down his mussed hair, which had grown uncharacteristically long. "Have safe travels."

He nodded. "You and the peanut stay safe, too."

"We will." Was he empty inside? His expression was void of emotion. If SEAL training included erasing all feeling, sign her up.

Knowing there was nothing left to say, she climbed behind the wheel of her car.

After a final, awkward wave, Deacon walked to his.

Ellie was too grounded in harsh reality to wish for Deacon to run back to her like men did in romantic movies. He'd made his choice. Her only task now was to figure out how to live with it.

"How HAVE YOU BEEN?" Helen asked at lunch a week after Deacon had left.

"Good," Ellie lied, but the restaurant's setting was so pretty, she didn't want to ruin their time together with more moping. Crystal Garden's wicker-and-glass dining tables had been set up in the hundred-year-old greenhouse of Fenmore Mansion, once the home of a steel tycoon, now a posh B and B. The redbrick floors provided an elegant foundation for tropical plants and birds. A tinkling trio of cherub fountains provided the perfect accompaniment to soft classical music. "But busy. You know how it is with a small child."

Wearing a wistful smile, Helen added artificial sweetener to her iced tea. "When Tom was little, there weren't so many outside distractions—no formalized play groups or nursery school. But we'd meet up with friends for fancy lunches in our homes. For a while, seems like all Tom and I did was dream up ways to outshine our neighbor, Peggy. I swear, that woman was nearly the death of me. If I had arrangements made of white daisies and snapdragons from the garden, she'd order white roses from the florist—a big deal back then."

"I'll bet." As much as Ellie wanted to be interested, she was too distracted by the truth of how abysmal her own life had been. "E-excuse me. I need to find the restroom."

Washing her hands a few minutes later, Ellie looked

into the mirror, then did a double take. Pandora, from Friends Helping Friends, stood before her, dressed in black slacks and a crisp white blouse. Her hair was neatly pulled back, and best of all, she appeared well-rested and sober. "Hi."

"Hey." They shared an awkward hug.

"You work here?" Ellie asked.

"Yeah. A friend got me the job. I've been at it for a month and really like it. Being around all the plants is nice."

"You look pretty. I hate to ask, but are you—"

"Still drinking?" Pandora shrugged. "Not as much, but every day is still a struggle."

"You could always come back to the center," Ellie offered. "I know I couldn't help you, but maybe someone else could."

"Look…" Through a misty smile, Pandora said, "I know you did your best to help, but you can't save everyone. My daughter's with a better family. I visit her every Saturday and the house she's in now is nicer than I could ever give her. Sure, I miss her like crazy, but that's my issue. She's happy, and that's all that really matters."

"But—"

"I don't mean to be rude," the woman said, "but I need to get back to work, and you need to learn to let things go. I'm in a good place. You should be, too."

Easier said than done.

Ironic, how Ellie went to the bathroom to pull herself together, but emerged feeling worse. At least Pandora's tables were on the opposite end of the restaurant from Ellie and Helen.

After more pointless small talk, Helen came right out

and asked, "Ever going to tell me what's really going on?"

"What do you mean?" Ellie pushed away her unfinished meal.

"You happen to love egg salad on a fresh-baked croissant, so when I see you looking at it as if it might as well be a worm, I know there's a problem." Softening her tone, Helen asked, "I hope there's nothing wrong with Pia?"

"She's great." Was now the time to go ahead and tell all? Ellie's meeting with Pandora had her feeling raw. As if the slightest emotional push would send her over the edge.

"Sweetheart? Are you crying?" Reaching for Ellie's hand, Helen urged, "Please tell me what has you down."

"I— It's Deacon. He's so great with Pia and I—I fell for him, only he wants nothing to do with me. I knew better, but couldn't stop myself. I feel like such a fool. Everything's a mess, and—"

"Shh…" Patting her shoulder, Helen told Ellie, "Deacon was always a handful. You may not want to hear this now, but I really think you not being with him is for the best."

"You've got a nice spread here." Deacon had grown to like horses on his last trip to Afghanistan. Blending in with the locals, riding had been a necessity. Now, sitting astride a palomino with seemingly all of south Texas spread before him, he should've been at peace. But in truth Deacon had never been more on edge. "All this space is a good thing."

Bowie grunted.

In the few days Deacon had spent with his mom and

biological father, he'd learned that his dad was a man of few words. When he did speak, it was usually only when he absolutely had to.

Bowie reined in his horse, leaning forward to smooth his paint's mane. "You ever gettin' to the heart of why you came all this way?"

"I thought it was for the two of us to get to know each other."

"Might be what you told yourself, but ask me?" He adjusted his cowboy hat to shade his dark eyes. "I think there's something more."

"No. I'm trying to figure out where to go from here. I had a lousy childhood and now—"

"Knock that crap off." Bowie reached into his denim shirt pocket for a can of Skoal. Pinching out a wad, he centered it between his lip and gums. "That's a cop-out. What's in the past is past. Not that I've met many SEALs, but I'm pretty sure that like my breed, yours don't quit." For a long time he sat silent, staring at the sun-and-shadow play on a far-off mesa. "Never told a soul, but I always hoped you and me might one day get acquainted. You probably won't believe this, but though you didn't know it, I've been with you since the day you were born." He reached into his saddlebag, handing Deacon a metal box. "I keep more up at the house. But this is the stuff that brings me the most solace."

Deacon took the tin, popped open the lid.

His throat tighter than it'd ever been, he fingered through newspaper clippings of his birth announcement, when he'd done good at an elementary science fair, later mentions of when he'd been in trouble with the local law. News of him joining the navy, earning his Trident and so much more. Photos of him from babyhood to the picture he'd recently sent his mom for Christmas. There were even a few snapshots of Pia.

Bowie asked, "You really prepared to be like your old man and let fear rob you of years with a good woman and your kid?"

"What do you mean?" Deacon asked hoarsely.

"I'm talking about this Ellie woman your mom tells me you've been mooning over. If I had it all to do over again, I'd have chucked my guilt over doing wrong by Clint and done everything within my power to move you and Peter in with me. Life's too short for regrets, son, and now that Sally is back in my life, as much as I loved my Nancy, I've realized we were more friends than lovers. Please..." He caught Deacon's gaze and held it. "I'm begging you, if there's only one thing you learn from me, if you know in your heart this Ellie is the right gal for you, hold on to her and never let go."

"It's not that simple."

"Sure it is." He spit. "Get a ring. Put it on her finger. That's all you have to do."

DEACON FINISHED OUT the week in Texas, the whole time wondering if his dad could be right. Had he been making his relationship with Ellie more complicated than it needed to be? How was he ever supposed to know?

He finished helping Bowie muck stalls and then sat down on the front steps of the ranch house, soaking in the afternoon sun. His old mutt, Cheesy, had come along with his mother in the move, and Deacon leaned sideways to pet the little guy. "Pretty nice here, huh?"

Deacon's family home had been in town, near the hospital. Out here, there were no sirens, only wind. It reminded him in ways of being on the water.

Cheesy wagged his tail, then scratched behind his ear. When he yelped, Deacon checked him out to find he'd caught his nail on his collar. It was a quick fix, and soon enough Cheesy was back to doing what he did best—nap. Deacon rubbed behind his ears awhile longer, then arched to stretch his back.

Only now he was the one wincing, when something in his pocket gave him a poke.

He fished around to figure out the problem, only to find the little plastic doll Pia always carried. He remembered she'd asked him to hold it for her the last time he was with her. Looking at that toy was like stepping into a time capsule. It served as such a simple, yet sweet reminder of how good it felt to be with his girls.

He'd wondered how he would know if being with Ellie and his daughter was the right thing for them all. Here was his answer in tangible form. Ridiculous that it'd taken such a seemingly insignificant thing to bring him around, but along with that clarity came peace. A sure sign he'd finally learned it didn't take a faultless pedigree to be a great father or husband, just love.

"WHAT ARE YOU DOING after we get out of here?" Ada asked Ellie fifteen minutes before closing the store.

"I'd like to take a nap, but I promised Pia we'd shop for Halloween."

"Why so early?" She tossed a blouse with a broken zipper on her desk in the office. "Don't you have almost the whole month left to shop?"

"Obviously, you don't have kids. Think of costume shopping as if Louis Vuitton was having a half-off sale, but for thirty days. By the end of the sale, nothing's left."

"Ah," Ada said with an exaggerated nod. "Now I understand. What's Pia going to be?"

"Last we talked, a pumpkin or Cinderella. Maybe if we—"

"Mommy!" The boutique's door opened and Pia raced in, hugging Ellie's legs and jumping. "I know secret!"

"How did you get here, sweetie? Did Nana Helen bring you?" Ellie looked toward the door, only to see an enormous bouquet of red roses attached to oh-so-familiar strong legs. *Deacon?*

"Daddy fun! We buy flowers! He love us!"
What?
Ellie was glad when Ada slipped her arm around her for support.

"Want me to stay or go?" her friend asked.

"S-stay." Deacon had already put Ellie through so much. Early on in their relationship, she'd been the one hurting him, but now? Emotionally, she'd become one big bruise.

"How's it going?" He set the roses on the counter. The rich scent enveloped her. He'd been gone only a week, yet her pulse raced as if he'd been off on another mission.

"Daddy, ring yet?" *Ring?* Pia was still jumping.

"Listen, uh…" Deacon looked at Ada. "Do you mind? I could use some privacy."

"Yeah, well, my friend could use some stability." The former model was nearly taller than him, and Ellie had her doubts as to who would win in a shouting match.

Ellie lifted Pia, settling her little girl on her hip. "Ada, I'll be all right, if you wouldn't mind handling closing?"

"Sure?" her friend asked.

Ellie nodded.

Deacon said, "My being here is no doubt a surprise, huh?"

"Yeah." Not in the mood for awkward small talk or games, she gestured for him to hurry up with whatever he felt he had to say. "Plus, Pia and I have a big night planned, so we need to get going. Thanks, though, for picking her up."

"You're not making this easy."

"What, Deacon? What could we possibly talk about that we haven't already been over a dozen times?"

"Now, Daddy?" Pia wriggled so much Ellie had a tough time holding her.

Tossing his hands up, Deacon said, "Why not? How could this go worse?"

"Look Mommy! Ring!" Pia held up the engagement ring Deacon had given her so long ago.

Ada popped out of her office. "Excuse me, just grabbing the cash drawer."

"Are you still open?" asked a rail-thin brunette at the door.

"Sure." Ada welcomed her inside. "Looking for anything in particular?"

Deacon swore under his breath. "Can we get out of here?"

Ellie glanced at Ada. "Are you all right on your own?"

Busy with her customer, she waved them on their way.

Outside, Deacon said, "This isn't going at all the way I planned. Wanna head to the beach?"

"I already told you I promised Pia to go costume shopping."

"Are you oblivious to my proposal? Geez, Ell, I just asked you to marry me. The least you could do is give me an answer."

"Correction—you had Pia hand me a ring. For all I know, you could've bought it for her. It wouldn't be your first inappropriate gift."

"Really? This is how you want this to go?" He looked so wounded, Ellie knew she'd gone too far.

She opened the car's rear door, tucking Pia into her safety seat. The little girl wore the ring on her thumb. Ellie took it. "If you are proposing to me, why here? Why now? What's changed to make you believe we're suddenly perfect for each other, when right after we made love, you proclaimed we were a bad idea?"

Raking his hand through his longish hair, he looked away. "How am I supposed to know why I did anything? You've changed me, Ell. For the better. Pia has, too. I was all messed up inside, but then this—" he withdrew Pia's tiny doll from his jeans pocket "—reminded me that no matter how far away from you two I am, all I want is to be with you again. I'm not good at this, so please, Ell, bear with me. I think I might love you—no, I know I do. And that's crazy to me, because I never even knew I was able to love, and—"

"Would you hush…" Hands to his chest, his ring on the appropriate finger, Ellie kissed him quiet. As far as proposals went, she'd seen far better in the movies, but that didn't matter. "What happened on this trip? I mean, besides you finding Pia's bootlegged doll? You do know she wasn't even supposed to have it? I think she took it from some kid at day care, and it refuses to disappear."

"Does it matter?" His latest kiss left her dizzy.

"Uh-huh." They kissed again. "Choking hazard."

"I don't mean to pressure you," he said, "but considering how many times we've almost been a couple, would you mind not waiting for the wedding?"

"This weekend works for me."

"Me, too," he said with a nuzzle to her neck. "I love you so freaking much. How could I not have known?"

"I love you, too." Only Ellie *had* known. She'd just been too afraid to give her feelings voice. What if he hadn't felt the same?

But he finally did. And the wait had been totally worth it.

* * * * *

Be sure to look for the next book in
Laura Marie Altom's
OPERATION: FAMILY *series,*
THE SEAL'S STOLEN CHILD,
available in December 2012!

REQUEST YOUR FREE BOOKS!
2 FREE NOVELS PLUS 2 FREE GIFTS!

♦ Harlequin®

American ★ *Romance*®

LOVE, HOME & HAPPINESS

YES! Please send me 2 FREE Harlequin® American Romance® novels and my 2 FREE gifts (gifts are worth about $10). After receiving them, if I don't wish to receive any more books, I can return the shipping statement marked "cancel." If I don't cancel, I will receive 4 brand-new novels every month and be billed just $4.49 per book in the U.S. or $5.24 per book in Canada. That's a saving of at least 14% off the cover price! It's quite a bargain! Shipping and handling is just 50¢ per book in the U.S. and 75¢ per book in Canada.* I understand that accepting the 2 free books and gifts places me under no obligation to buy anything. I can always return a shipment and cancel at any time. Even if I never buy another book, the two free books and gifts are mine to keep forever.

154/354 HDN FEP2

Name _____ (PLEASE PRINT)

Address _____ Apt. #

City _____ State/Prov. _____ Zip/Postal Code

Signature (if under 18, a parent or guardian must sign)

Mail to the **Reader Service:**
IN U.S.A.: P.O. Box 1867, Buffalo, NY 14240-1867
IN CANADA: P.O. Box 609, Fort Erie, Ontario L2A 5X3

Not valid for current subscribers to Harlequin American Romance books.

Want to try two free books from another line?
Call 1-800-873-8635 or visit www.ReaderService.com.

* Terms and prices subject to change without notice. Prices do not include applicable taxes. Sales tax applicable in N.Y. Canadian residents will be charged applicable taxes. Offer not valid in Quebec. This offer is limited to one order per household. All orders subject to credit approval. Credit or debit balances in a customer's account(s) may be offset by any other outstanding balance owed by or to the customer. Please allow 4 to 6 weeks for delivery. Offer available while quantities last.

Your Privacy—The Reader Service is committed to protecting your privacy. Our Privacy Policy is available online at www.ReaderService.com or upon request from the Reader Service.

We make a portion of our mailing list available to reputable third parties that offer products we believe may interest you. If you prefer that we not exchange your name with third parties, or if you wish to clarify or modify your communication preferences, please visit us at www.ReaderService.com/consumerschoice or write to us at Reader Service Preference Service, P.O. Box 9062, Buffalo, NY 14269. Include your complete name and address.

HAR11B

*Welcome to the Texas Hill Country! In the third book
in Tanya Michaels's series* **HILL COUNTRY HEROES,**
*a desperate mother is in hiding with her little girl.
The last thing she needs is her nosy Texas Ranger
neighbor getting friendly....*

Alex raised her gaze, starting to say something, but then
she froze like a possum in oncoming headlights.

"Mrs. Hunt? Everything okay?"

She eyed the encircled silver star pinned to his denim
button-down shirt. He'd been working this morning and
hadn't bothered to remove the badge. "Interesting symbol,"
she said slowly.

"Represents the Texas Rangers."

"L-like the baseball team?"

"No, ma'am. Like the law enforcement agency." Maybe
that would make her feel safer about her temporary new
surroundings. He jerked his thumb toward his house. "You
have a bona fide lawman living right next door."

Beneath the freckles, her face went whiter than his hat.
"Really? That's…" She gave herself a quick shake. "Come
on, Belle. Inside now. Before, um, before that mud stains."

"Okay." Belle hung her head but rallied long enough to add,
"Bye-bye, Mister Zane. I hope I get to pet Dolly again soon."

From Alex's behavior, Zane had a suspicion they
wouldn't be getting together for neighborly potluck din-
ners anytime in the near future. Instead of commenting on
the kid's likelihood of seeing Dolly again, he waved. "Bye,
Belle. Stay fabulous."

She beamed. "I will!"

Then mother and daughter disappeared into the house,
the front door banging shut behind them.

"Is there something about me," he asked Dolly, "that makes females want to slam doors?"

The only response he got from the dog was an impatient tug on her leash. "Right. I promised you a walk." They started again down the sidewalk, but he found himself periodically glancing over his shoulder and pondering his new neighbors. Cute kid, but she seemed like a handful. And Alex Hunt, once she'd calmed from her mama-bear fury, was perhaps the most skittish woman he'd ever met. If she were a horse, she'd have to wear blinders to keep from jumping at her own shadow. Zane wondered if there was a Mr. Hunt in the picture.

Be sure to look for RESCUED BY A RANGER by Tanya Michaels in September 2012 from Harlequin® American Romance®!